"You know what your problem is?"

Five minutes and already Luke was going to tell her what her problems were! Her defenses instantly went up.

"No," she snapped, "but I have a feeling you're about to tell me!"

"Your problem is you're used to dealing with little boys who pretend to be men." His voice dropped to a husky whisper. "I'm not your little brother, Kati. I'm a man."

"A man," she repeated dully. The word echoed through her mind, and she couldn't help but wonder how on earth such a harmless word could suddenly sound so ominous.

"Yes, Kati," he said. "A man." The big callused hands that had so gently stroked her hair slipped around her waist, pulling her closer.

It was wrong, her mind screamed, but her body and senses paid no attention. Guilt and fear evaporated like fog on a misty morning as Luke's lips gently lowered over hers.

Dear Reader:

The spirit of the Silhouette Romance Homecoming Celebration lives on as each month we bring you six books by continuing stars!

And we have a galaxy of stars planned for 1988. In the coming months, we're publishing romances by many of your favorite authors such as Annette Broadrick, Sondra Stanford and Brittany Young. Beginning in January, Debbie Macomber has written a trilogy designed to cure any midwinter blues. And that's not all—during the summer, Diana Palmer presents her most engaging heros and heroines in a trilogy that will be sure to capture your heart.

Your response to these authors and other authors of Silhouette Romances has served as a touchstone for us, and we're pleased to bring you more books with Silhouette's distinctive medley of charm, wit and—above all—romance.

I hope you enjoy this book and the many stories to come. Come home to romance—for always!

Sincerely,

Tara Hughes
Senior Editor
Silhouette Books

SHARON DE VITA

Kane and Mabel

Silhouette Romance

Published by Silhouette Books New York

America's Publisher of Contemporary Romance

This book is dedicated with love to Margaret Higgins
Pelligrino—wife, mother, attorney, friend and . . . the
most courageous lady I know. We've come a long
way from that sunny day on the *Summer Wind* when
writing was just a dream.
This one's for you, Peg.

SILHOUETTE BOOKS
300 E. 42nd St., New York, N.Y. 10017

Copyright © 1987 by Sharon De Vita

ISBN: 0-373-08545-1

First Silhouette Books printing December 1987

Books by Sharon De Vita

Silhouette Romance

Heavenly Match #475
Lady and the Legend #498
Kane and Mabel #545

SHARON DE VITA

decided around her thirtieth birthday that she wanted
to produce something that didn't have to be walked or
fed during the night. An eternal optimist who always
believes in happy endings, she felt romances were the
perfect vehicle for her creative energies. As a reader,
and a writer, she prefers stories that are fun and light-
hearted, and tries to inject these qualities in the stories
she writes. The mother of three, she has been happily
married to her high school sweetheart for eighteen
years.

IOWA

NEBRASKA

ILLINOIS

Libertyville

KANSAS • Kansas City

Missouri River

St. Louis

MISSOURI

Underlined places are fictitious.

N

ARKANSAS

Chapter One

"Lordy, Kati Rose, you'd better come quick! All hell's broke loose!" Bessie's voice edged up in panic as she skidded through the swinging doors that led into the kitchen.

"Now what?" Kati asked, looking up from the custard she was mixing.

"Mr. Billings and Vera are at it again! She's hollering her lungs loose because he brought that old hound dog in with him. She's threatening to call the health inspector!"

"Again!" Kati sighed in exasperation. "What did you tell her?"

"I told her to quit her jawing before her false teeth fell out."

"That was very diplomatic of you, Bessie," Kati said, ducking her head to hide a smile.

"Don't know what she's yapping about. Poor Beauregard's too old to bother anybody. Besides," Bessie huffed, "he's got a better disposition than Vera will ever have."

"And I suppose," Kati inquired, arching one auburn brow, "that you found it necessary to point that out to her?"

"Sure did," Bessie proclaimed proudly. "It's the truth, ain't it? Oh, and I almost forgot, there's a handsome cuss out front, says he's a friend of your brother's. He's asking a whole lot of questions 'bout the diner. Not that you can hear him too well with all the commotion going on."

"A friend of Patrick's?" Kati asked in alarm. "What did you tell him?"

"I didn't tell him anything!" Bessie announced, clearly insulted that Kati would even think such a thing.

Sighing, Kati shook her head in exasperation. "Bessie, I don't have time for this nonsense today. The meeting at the bank took longer than I expected, and I never had a chance to talk to anyone about that extension on my loan. I'll take care of Vera and Mr. Billings. As for the stranger, I've had my fill of Patrick's freeloading friends. The last one that was here helped himself to almost four hundred dollars. *My four hundred dollars.* And the one before him thought I was running a free boarding house. It almost took an act of Congress to get rid of him. Patrick may own half this diner, but I'm the one running it, and worrying about it." Sighing, Kati set the pan of custard into a bowl of warm water and slid it into the oven. "This blasted oven," she complained, popping the temperamental door closed with her knee. "Now." She turned her attention to Bessie, absently wiping her hands on her apron. "I don't have time to put up with any more of Patrick's freeloading friends. You'll just have to get rid of him."

"No, sir," Bessie said firmly, shaking her gray head. "Not me. I've seen his kind before. I'd rather tangle with Vera."

Kati looked at her in surprise. "What's so special about this one?"

Bessie shifted her ample frame uncomfortably. "Well, for one thing, his voice sounds like it rumbled over from the next county, and for another...well, you'd better just come have a look."

Muttering under her breath at this latest complication, Kati marched across the spotless kitchen to peer through the window of the swinging door.

Chaos would hardly describe the scene. Vera, dressed impeccably as always in a suit, hat and gloves, was engaged in a heated debate with Mr. Billings, who was cradling the poor hound dog in his arms, out of harm's way and Vera's reach. Kati scanned the diner. It was then that she saw him. Even sitting down, he was too darn big to miss.

Her enormous emerald eyes widened and the hair on the back of her neck stood on end. "Damnation!"

"I told you so, Kati," Bessie said smugly, trying to peek over Kati's shoulder.

Lord, he was big. And broad, and deeply bronzed, with a shock of black hair that tumbled recklessly around an exceptionally handsome face. A blue work shirt stretched tautly across shoulders that looked a mile wide. Faded denim covered legs that seemed to go on forever. Kati inched upward, stretching her spine so she could see the rest of him. Lord, she thought, her eyes widening, his booted feet looked like snowshoes! She suddenly understood Bessie's reluctance to tangle with the man. Self-preservation was high on her list, also.

He was undoubtedly the most attractive man Kati had ever seen, but that didn't stop her temper from flaring. She didn't need another freeloader looking for cash, or a place to crash. Handsome or not, she fully intended to get rid of him. Pronto.

"Think he's looking to borrow money?" Bessie whispered.

Kati shook her head. "I'm not sure and even if he is, he's out of luck. He'll just have to step to the back of the line. If I don't get an extension on that loan..." Kati chewed her bottom lip. "I'm almost two months behind on the mortgage payment now, thanks to Patrick's sticky-fingered friend!"

"What are we going to do?"

"*We're* going to find out what he wants," Kati announced, yanking off her apron and dropping it to a heap on the gleaming counter. "But first we have to separate Mr. Billings and Vera." Dragging a hand through her auburn hair, Kati pushed through the swinging door with Bessie right on her heels.

"Mr. Billings," Kati called, ignoring the stranger for a moment. "Your egg custard will be ready in about an hour. Why don't you take Beauregard to the park? If you bring him around back, I'll have Bessie give him a nice bone."

Mr. Billings tried to squeeze out of the booth past Vera who refused to budge. Hands on hips, Vera stood firmly planted in front of him.

"Kati Rose!" Vera's high-pitched whine scratched at Kati's nerve endings. "How do you expect decent folks to enjoy their meal when you allow that over-grown rodent free rein in your establishment? Never seen such conduct in all my born days." Vera sighed dramatically. "Why, when I was in the theater in New York—a civilized city, mind you—this type of behavior would never be allowed."

"Theater!" Mr. Billings gave a loud snort and glared at Vera over the top of his spectacles. "The closest you ever came to the theater, Vera Wilson, was selling popcorn at the movies on Saturday afternoon. And who are you calling a *rodent*?" he yelled, pushing his nose into Vera's startled face.

"How dare you!" Vera cried, fluttering her hand to her forehead. "How dare you speak to me like that. You—you—opprobrious heathen!"

"What'd she call me?" he asked Kati out of the side of his mouth.

"Now, now," Kati soothed, trying to hang on to her patience. "I'm sure we can settle this. There's no sense saying things we'll be sorry for later." Out of the corner of her eye, Kati saw the stranger slide off his stool and head in her direction. Instantly annoyed, she turned pleading eyes toward Bessie. She could only handle one problem at a time.

"You gotta wait your turn," Bessie told the man, giving him a good poke in the arm in case he hadn't heard her. She hustled him to a booth and poured him a cup of coffee.

Kati dragged her eyes from him, sanity overruling her curiosity. Vera and Mr. Billings were playing tug-of-war with the poor dog.

"That's enough," Kati yelled, causing the two of them to stop and gape at her.

"There's certainly no reason to raise your voice, Kati Rose," Vera scolded, fluffing her hair indignantly. "Letting animals in here, and now raising your voice. I don't know what's come over you lately. Ever since that brother of yours ran off leaving you to work the diner, you've been mighty testy."

"I agree with you, Vera." Mr. Billings nodded his head and turned his gaze toward Kati. "You know you have been mighty cranky lately."

Mr. Billings patted Vera's arm. "Bo and I are going for a walk. Would you care to join us?" He nodded his head toward Kati and lowered his voice. "We'll come back when *she's* not feeling quite so peaked."

"Why, Mr. Billings," Vera preened, "how kind of you to ask. I do believe I'd like that. Did you know in Europe, animals are allowed everywhere?" Vera giggled girlishly and Kati rolled her eyes. These two fought like cats and dogs almost every day, yet let someone come between them and they'd stick together like flies to glue.

After taking Mr. Billings' arm Vera turned to Kati, her eyes soft and full of sympathy. "Perhaps you should consider meditating, dear. It will free your body of all hostilities. It's not good for you to keep everything boiling up inside." Vera's eyes grew dreamy and she sighed in remembrance. "It's a trick I learned from one of my acting teachers while I was in New York. I studied with the best, you know." She patted Kati's cheek. "Try it, dear, you'll see. It will cleanse your spirit and soothe your Karma." With an airy wave Vera and Mr. Billings sailed out the door, leaving Kati shaking her head.

"What's wrong?" Bessie asked from behind, causing Kati to jump.

"My hostilities are boiling in my Karma," she muttered under her breath.

"Makes sense to me." Bessie nodded toward the stranger. "One problem down. One to go."

Kati's emerald eyes widened and she looked at him suspiciously. He was lounging in the booth as if he belonged here! She was going to make short work of him today, she thought darkly.

"Go check the custard," Kati instructed Bessie, moving toward the man. "I'll get rid of *him*." Pushing back a tumble of auburn curls, Kati approached him warily, stopping a good distance from the booth.

"Can I help you?"

He lifted his head and Kati found herself staring into the most glorious blue eyes she had ever seen. He was more attractive up close than she'd anticipated. Her mouth grew dry as his gaze slowly swept over her, from the top of her unruly auburn curls, across the white blouse and past the faded jeans to linger on her tattered sneakers.

A smile twitched at his mouth. "A little more coffee would be nice." He lifted his cup to her and Kati glared at him. Another freeloader, she knew it! If she started waiting on him and serving him free food, she'd never get rid of him.

Yanking the cup out of his hand, Kati stormed behind the counter, and grabbed the pot left over from breakfast. Sloshing some cold coffee into his cup, she returned to the booth, and banged the cup down in front of him. Tapping her foot impatiently and trying not to stare at him, she waited while he took a sip.

"This coffee is terrible," he announced, and Kati reached out and snatched the cup out of his hand.

"Since you don't want any more of my coffee, perhaps you'll tell me what you do want?"

One black brow rose and his eyes danced merrily. "Do you treat all your customers so courteously?" he asked casually, pausing to roll up the sleeves of his shirt.

"Listen Mr.—"

"Kane. Lucas Kane." He held out his hand and Kati stared at it as if it were a snake ready to strike. Her eyes caught a flash of something on his arm. A tattoo, that much she knew for sure. She tried not to stare, but her curiosity got the best of her and she squinted, trying to make out the words.

"Born To Raise Kane," he drawled slowly, and Kati's startled gaze flew to his. Her breath caught unexpectedly and she felt annoyance streak through her.

"Mr. Kane," she said sharply. "I have work to do, so if you don't mind, would you please state what your business with my brother is, so that I can get on with *my* business?"

"Ahhh, my business. Well, Mabel . . ." Leaning back against the booth he inclined his head to study her from a different angle.

"My name's not Mabel," she snapped, a little off balance at the way he was looking at her.

He frowned in obvious confusion. "Who's Mabel?" he inquired, and Kati ground her teeth. Just because the diner was called Mabel's didn't mean there had to *be* a Mabel. That was the name of the diner when she purchased it. She bought the place from a man named Bruno, and he'd never seen hide nor hair of anyone named Mabel, either. Everyone in town knew who really owned the place, so there didn't seem much point in changing the name. Besides, new signs cost money, money better spent elsewhere, not that she intended to explain all of that to him.

"Would you please state your business?" Kati demanded, her patience sorely strained.

He smiled pleasantly. "I guess you could say my business is your business." Kati narrowed her eyes to stare at him suspiciously.

"What the devil are you talking about, Mr. Kane? I don't have time to play guessing games with you."

"Call me Luke."

"I'll call you a lot more than that if you don't hurry up and tell me what you want!" Kati threatened, trying to ignore Bessie who was waving frantically from the kitchen.

He lifted his finger and beckoned Kati closer. Puzzled, but anxious to learn what he wanted, she leaned down so he could whisper in her ear. "You know," he said softly, his warm breath fanning her hair, "you *are* mighty testy. Perhaps you should try meditating. Maybe your Karma *is* out of whack!"

Jerking upright, Kati glared at him, not at all amused by the mischief in his eyes. "What do you want?"

"Food," he said simply. "But after that coffee, I don't know if I should risk it. I'm not too fond of food poisoning."

"Food poisoning!" Kati bellowed, glaring at the man. How dare he insult her diner. "I'll have you know the food in here is excellent. Not that *you're* going to get any of it!"

"Kati Rose!" Bessie hurried in from the kitchen, rolling her eyes and jerking her head backward to let Kati know that Everett, the president of the town's only bank, was right behind her. "Everett's here. Says he got your message and he wants to talk to you."

Everett cleared his throat as his eyes connected with Luke. Kati wasn't sure if it was her imagination or not, but the dour banker seemed to pale at the sight of the handsome stranger. Handsome, large stranger, Kati amended silently.

"Afternoon, Kati Rose. I'm sorry I missed you this morning. Had important banking business that needed tending to." Everett glanced quickly at Luke, and then back at her. "Could we sit down and talk?"

Kati smiled warmly and took Everett's arm. Everything was riding on this meeting. Everett was a proper man who took his banking business seriously. Somehow, she had to convince him to give her an extension on her loan. Kati guided him to the next booth away from Lucas Kane's prying eyes—and ears.

"Could I have a ham sandwich and a fresh cup of coffee?" Luke asked Bessie. Kati whipped her head around.

"No, you cannot have a ham sandwich and a cup of coffee," she hissed, glaring at him. Luke smiled, not at all fazed by her annoyance.

Everett slid into the booth and sighed. "What a day it's been, Kati. A cup of your coffee might be nice."

"Don't you dare give that man anything," Kati instructed Bessie, pointing to Luke.

"Excuse me?" Everett was frowning and Kati reached out and patted his hand.

"I wasn't talking about you, Everett. Now, what were you saying?"

"Why can't I have a sandwich?" Luke asked her from behind.

"Do you mind?" Kati whispered fiercely, turning to give him a look that should have felled him on the spot. "I'm trying to have a private conversation here. A conversation that has nothing to do with you."

"Kati, are you listening to me?" Everett was looking at her strangely and she tried to give him her full attention. It was hard with Luke breathing down her neck.

"If I apologize for insulting your cooking," Luke whispered hopefully, "then can I have a sandwich?"

Kati pretended not to hear him. "Go on," she urged Everett with a smile, trying to ignore the warmth shimmying down her neck from Lucas Kane's closeness. "I'm listening to you."

"Kati, I'm not certain we can give you another extension. You're already two months behind as it is." Everett looked at her sadly and Kati's nerves tightened.

"I'm sorry," Luke said in her ear, sounding anything but. "Did you know you smelled like vanilla?" he whispered huskily, inhaling deeply. "It's nice. I like it."

Feeling unaccountably flustered, Kati turned to glare at him, and was caught up short by his nearness. Her pulse quickened. Luke was so close she could see the mischief dancing in his eyes, see the laugh lines etched around his full mouth. What a nice mouth, she thought distractedly, then quickly rechanneled her thoughts.

"Would you please quit sniffing me?" she hissed. With that, she snapped her head around and tried to pay attention to Everett. It was difficult.

"I'm sorry, Kati Rose," the banker said, closing his briefcase. "You do understand, don't you?"

"Since I've already apologized, now can I have my sandwich?" Luke asked hopefully.

"No!" she bellowed, hitting the table with her fist. "You can apologize until hell freezes over! But it won't—" Kati stopped abruptly and her eyes widened in alarm. "No, Everett, wait—please—I wasn't talking to you. Honest. I was talking to him!" Kati jumped up and whirled, pointing to Luke, but it was too late.

Everett was gathering up his papers, his chin set in a defiant angle. "Kati, I have tried very hard to be patient during these trying financial times. I know it's been hard since your brother left; but really, I think your attitude needs to be improved." Scowling, Everett bolted from the booth and hurried toward the door with his briefcase *and* Kati's papers clutched in his hands.

Remorsefully she watched him slam out of the diner. Everett was gone, along with her only chance for saving the diner.

Clenching her teeth, she turned and advanced toward Luke. "You!" she seethed. "Are you happy now?"

"I'd be happier if I had something to eat," Luke grumbled.

"Do you know what you've just done?" Kati bellowed, raising her fist in his general direction, and wondering if a knuckle sandwich would satisfy his appetite. "You have single-handedly ruined my business!"

"Ruined your business?" Luke frowned. "All *I* did was ask for a sandwich." Dark brows gathered over confused blue eyes. "Who was that guy, anyway?"

"Not that it's any of your concern, Mr. Kane, but *that* was the president of the bank. And because of you, I probably won't get an extension on my loan!" Kati knew full well that it really wasn't Lucas Kane's fault. But he was just the closest, most convenient person to vent her anger and frustration on. Without that extension on her loan, she knew she was probably going to lose her business. The thought filled her with anger.

"Is that all? Why didn't you say so?" Luke slid from the booth and started toward the front door. "I'll be right back."

"Oh no, you won't," Kati called after him. "If you show your face in my diner again I'll have you arrested for trespassing," she threatened, slamming the door shut firmly behind him.

"Kati?" Bessie called hesitantly.

"What!"

"No need to get huffy with me," Bessie scolded. "I just wanted to know if I should check the custard?"

Rubbing her temples, Kati sighed heavily. No sense taking out her frustrations on Bessie. "I'm sorry," she said, dragging up a smile. "Yes, would you please go check the custard?"

A moment later Bessie was back, muttering under her breath. "I checked it."

One auburn brow rose. "And?"

"It's burnt," Bessie confirmed, bobbing her head. "I told you we had to get that oven fixed."

"Damnation!" Kati muttered, storming through to the kitchen. She flipped off the gas, grabbed a mitt, pulled the charred mess out of the oven and dumped it into the garbage.

"Bessie!"

The woman puffed into the kitchen, clutching her chest. "Now what!"

"Do you still have your shotgun?"

Bessie frowned. "Why you asking?"

"If that man Kane shows his face in my diner again, I want you to shoot him. Understand?"

Bessie looked at her skeptically. "You're the boss. What did that fellow want anyway?"

"A sandwich," Kati growled, snatching ingredients out of the refrigerator to make another batch of egg custard before Mr. Billings came back.

Bessie scratched her gray head. "All that Kane fellow wanted was a sandwich, but if he comes back, you want me to shoot him?"

Ignoring the look on Bessie's face, Kati slammed a bowl on the counter. "You got it."

"I see." Bessie stuffed her hands into the pockets of her apron and rocked back and forth on her heels. "Now

I know you don't like being told what to do, Kati Rose, but don't you think business might slack off a bit if word gets out you're shooting the customers?''

Kati's head snapped up and she pursed her lips together. "Bessie," she said slowly, "don't you have the evening set-ups to do?"

"I'm on my way." Whistling softly, Bessie swung out of the kitchen.

Taking a deep breath to compose herself, Kati took her frustration out on the hapless custard, whipping it furiously with a wooden spoon. The minute Bessie told her that someone was asking about Patrick she should have known it would be trouble. Any friend of her brother's usually was. She didn't mind Patrick up and leaving her to run the diner all alone. She'd been expecting it. In a way, it was her own fault. Five years older than he, she'd raised him after their parents' death, using the little bit of money that was willed to them to buy the diner.

She'd tried to make up for their parents' death by giving Patrick everything he wanted, giving in to his every whim. As a result, Patrick had grown up totally irresponsible and very self-centered. She had no one to blame but herself. Out of love, she had created a totally selfish individual. She'd been kind and patient with her brother in the past, but enough was enough! Patrick was twenty-two now, and it was time he stood on his own two feet. That was why he left in the first place. He found the small town of Libertyville, Missouri, boring, and owning a diner unexciting. He set off to seek his fortune, leaving her to run the diner. In some ways it had been easier for her after Patrick left. Oh, she missed him terribly, but at least she didn't have to worry about looking after him anymore, or bailing him out of trouble. Until his friends started showing up. She had spoiled her brother; she wasn't about to start extending the courtesy to his friends.

A rapid knock sounded at the back door just as she slipped the new batch of custard into the oven.

"Come on in, Mr. Billings," she called, pushing her hair off her face. "The custard's not quite ready yet, but I'll pour you some fresh coffee while you wait."

"How come he can have fresh coffee but I can't?" asked a surprisingly familiar voice and Kati sucked in her breath.

"You!" She whirled to face him. "What are you doing here? Get out right now!" Kati advanced toward him brandishing the wooden spoon in his direction.

"Now hold on a minute, I've got something for you." Luke waved a piece of paper under her nose and Kati swiped it in half with the spoon.

"Out!" she bellowed. "You've been here less than an hour and have caused me nothing but trouble."

Leaning close, he flashed her a dazzling smile. "Honey," he whispered huskily, causing her pulse to jump like a frog in flight, "even *I* need more than an hour to get into trouble."

"Bessie!" Kati backed him up against the refrigerator. "Get me your gun!"

Bessie skidded into the kitchen, took one look at Luke and shook her head. "Son," she sighed, "if I were you, I'd make a run for it."

"Here." Luke thrust his half of the paper at Bessie. "Read this."

Her eyes scanned the paper. "Lordy, Kati, it's some kind of receipt. Looks like it's from Everett."

"What? Let me see that!" Kati snatched the paper from Bessie's hand, her mind not believing what her eyes were reading. Lucas Kane had paid her past due mortgage payments. "All right, Kane, what's your gimmick?" she demanded.

"It's no gimmick. I was simply protecting my investment." Luke crossed his arms over his chest as Kati's eyes narrowed.

"What do you mean, protecting your investment?"

"It's a long story."

"Shorten it!" she demanded, shaking the spoon at him again.

"Your brother Patrick and I went into a business deal together and—"

"Lordy!" Bessie sighed loudly and shook her head. "And I thought *you looked like a smart one*." Her mouth snapped closed as Kati and Luke turned to stare at her.

"Go on," Kati urged.

"It's very simple." Luke shrugged and flashed her a smile. "Your brother put up his half of this diner as collateral."

Kati blinked rapidly. "What are you saying?"

"What I'm saying," Luke said softly, reaching out to pluck the spoon from her grasp, "is that I'm your new partner!"

Chapter Two

Kati's mouth fell open and for the first time in her life, she was speechless. She stared at Luke as if he had just grown another head. Forcing her lungs to work, Kati inhaled deeply, stiffened her spine and thrust her shoulders back.

"Like hell you are!" she roared, causing Luke to burst into laughter which only infuriated her further.

"You're Patrick's sister, all right!" He fished in his pocket and waved a piece of paper at her. "Here it is in black and white."

Glaring up at him, Kati ripped the paper from his hand and studied it carefully. There was no denying the signature was Patrick's. And from the jumbled legal document, she had a sinking feeling the paper was as real as the man standing before her. She raised her startled green eyes to his.

"I don't believe it," she whispered, shock causing her words to come out in short, jerky gasps. Patrick had

done some dastardly deeds, but this was unconsciona-
ble. She lowered her eyes to the paper in front of her
again, and the words began to blur as Kati's legs turned
to rubber.

"It's not possible," she whispered, tightening her fingers on the paper until it was crumpled into a tiny ball.
"It's just not possible."

"Lordy," Bessie whimpered. "I better go get the spirits."

Luke caught Kati around the waist and lowered her
gently into a nearby chair. She was trembling and her
enormous green eyes were shadowed in fear. Something
sudden and unexpected tugged at his heart, and he cursed
Patrick Ryan under his breath.

"Here." Bessie rushed back in and thrust a bottle of
amber-colored liquid at Luke. "Give her a good snort of
this."

Taking the bottle, Luke poured a little of the liquid
into a cup and handed it to Kati. For a moment she simply stared at it. His hand was large and callused, with
long, thick fingers. A nice hand, she thought dully, before her senses righted.

"I don't want that," she stammered, pushing the cup
away and trying to take a deep breath.

"Drink it!" Luke ordered, pressing the glass into her
shaking hands.

Irritated, but too stunned to resist, Kati give him a
black look before taking the cup. She stared at the dark
liquid, her thoughts tangled. How could Patrick do this
to her? she wondered as she raised the glass to her lips
and took a large gulp.

She clenched her eyes tightly shut as the liquor burned
a path down the back of her throat, exploding into a
thousand warm fingers in her empty belly. Gasping for

air, Kati tried to breathe, but found all she could manage was a raspy wheeze. Luke reached down and whacked her several times on the back.

Maybe she should have shot him when she had the chance, she thought miserably, as he pried the glass loose from her hand.

"Feeling better?" Luke inquired, kneeling down next to her. His blue eyes searched hers and Kati stared at him blankly.

"Better?" she whispered, raising her resentful eyes to his. "Better? You pour liquor down my throat, smack me on the back, threaten to take my diner away and you want to know if I'm feeling better?" She jumped to her feet. "And to make matters worse," Kati grumbled, fighting back tears, "I don't even drink!"

She spun away from him, not wanting to let on how upset she really was. The enormity of the situation hit her. Hot salty tears stung her eyes, but she swallowed them back. She'd die before she let Lucas Kane see them. Snatching her apron off the counter, Kati fumbled with the ties, trying to get the blasted thing around her.

"Here, let me." Luke slid his arms around her waist and adjusted the apron correctly. Swallowing the lump lodged in her throat, Kati took a deep, calming breath.

"Mr. Kane," she said coldly, not trusting herself to turn and face him. "I've got work to do. I'd appreciate it if you'd get out of my way!" Whirling, she began moving around the kitchen, trying to think and to put some distance between her and Luke.

Luke watched her in silence, occasionally moving out of her way when she needed to get into the refrigerator or into a cabinet. He decided to let her have a few minutes to herself. Give her a chance to digest his presence.

His eyes followed her and he resisted a smile. She sure as hell was a surprise. A bit of a spitfire with those fiery emerald eyes and that wild mass of auburn curls. Not much bigger than a nickel, she was about as friendly as a wounded yak. But she sure could hold her own, he thought with sudden admiration.

He was more intrigued by her than he cared to admit. She was so different from the women he knew. Strong, spirited and fiercely independent. If he had to, he'd bet everything he owned she didn't have a spot of makeup on. Her skin was smooth and soft, just begging to be touched. And that hair of hers, curly as a lamb, and much too silky to come out of any coloring bottle. No flowery perfume for her either, he mused silently. She smelled of warmth and sweetness...and vanilla. A smile broke loose—quite a combination.

Obviously his sudden appearance was a shock to her. Luke glanced around the gleaming kitchen. Not any more of a shock than this place turned out to be. Patrick Ryan had sure sold him a bill of goods. Luke's smile broadened. He would have been angry if it wasn't so darn funny. Lucas Kane getting taken by a twenty-two-year-old kid!

"Only restaurant in town," Patrick had told him. "A virtual gold mine. Jammed every day and worth every penny." Luke had believed him. Even though Patrick Ryan had been a bit irresponsible in the few short months he had worked for Luke, there was something about the kid that Luke had liked. When Patrick had come to him for a loan using the diner as collateral, Luke had been hesitant at first. Hell, what did he know about the restaurant business? He was a construction man. The closest he had ever come to a restaurant was as a customer.

Patrick had been persuasive, it was a sure deal. Guaranteed. Luke had more money than he'd ever need, and the idea of helping the kid out appealed to him. There was something about Patrick that was familiar, but it wasn't until later that Luke had finally figured it out. Besides, he reasoned, everyone needed a break once in his life. Luke shifted his frame, remembering his first break.

He'd been a wild sixteen-year-old, running from the law and the latest foster home the night he broke into Leonard Kane's construction trailer. Leonard was a gruff old man, all alone like Luke. After nearly scaring the life out of Luke, Leonard gave him a home and a job, and then eventually his name. Luke never forgot it. The old man had given him the one thing he'd never had: love. Someone to care about, someone to call his own. He finally belonged somewhere. That first break had made a difference in *his* life.

The familiarity of Patrick Ryan had been bugging him, and it wasn't until he went through some of Leonard's old papers that he understood why. Sean Ryan, Patrick's father, had been a business acquaintance of Leonard's. And judging from the cancelled loan papers Luke had found, Sean had bailed Leonard out of a jam years ago. Luke realized then and there, no matter what, he owed it to Leonard's memory, to the goodness of the man who had loved him and treated him like a son, to help Patrick out. Maybe Leonard was gone now, but there was no reason Luke couldn't pass on the kindness the man had extended to him.

So he had given Patrick money. But Patrick had disappeared, taking Luke's cash with him. The way Luke figured, sooner or later, no doubt when his money ran out, the kid would have to come back to Libertyville. And Luke would be waiting for him.

Now all he had to do was figure out a way to persuade *Kati* to let him stay. No easy task, he realized suddenly as she turned to give him a frosty look.

"Are you going to stand there getting in my way all day?" Kati demanded when her patience had run thin.

"No," Luke said quietly. "I'm just waiting for you to stand still long enough for me to talk to you, Kati."

The last thing she wanted to do was give him a chance to talk. She wasn't interested in anything he had to say, unless of course it was goodbye. Ignoring his comment, Kati reached around him to grab a pan, but Luke caught her arm. His fingers were warm, and his touch sent a tingle through her. Kati snatched her arm free. She wasn't particularly fond of the way her innards reacted to his nearness.

"In case you haven't noticed, *Mr. Kane*," she said his name with as much regret as she could muster, "I have work to do."

"*We*," he corrected, his eyes lit with humor, "have work to do." Luke reached up and grabbed another apron off the hook and slipped it around his waist. "And since we're partners, the least you can do is call me Luke."

Swallowing back the few words she'd really like to call him, Kati glared at him, annoyed at his good humor, and just annoyed in general. What started out as a bad day had suddenly turned worse, all because of this man. And her brother. When she got her hands on Patrick..."

"Just tell me what to do, Kati," he said pleasantly. "I'm sure I can be helpful."

"Helpful!" Her eyes widened in stunned anger. The nerve of the man! "And what exactly do *you* know about running a diner, Mr. Kane?"

"Not much," he admitted, smiling into her resentful green eyes. "But it can't be that hard. Besides, I'm a quick learner and I'm sure you'll be able to teach me what I need to know."

"Teach you!" she sputtered, poking a finger into his chest. "I have neither the time nor the inclination to teach *you* anything. I have a business to run."

"*We*," he corrected again, unaware of the inner turmoil he was causing her. "*We* have a business to run." Luke glanced quickly around the kitchen. "Perhaps I can be useful in other ways?"

"I appreciate your offer of help," Kati said sarcastically, her aggravation clearly evident. "But the only way you can be useful is to leave. The sooner the better."

"You want me to leave?" Luke feigned shock, but she didn't miss the humor dancing in his eyes. Why did she get the feeling he was up to something?

"Yes, the sooner the better."

"Well, Kati," Luke said on a long sigh, "I guess I don't have any other choice."

Kati's shoulders slumped in relief, and her sigh echoed around the kitchen. She had no idea it would be so easy to get rid of Lucas Kane. Not that she didn't feel just a bit sorry for him. But just because he had entered into a business deal with her brother was no reason for *her* to be saddled with him. She didn't have the time or the patience to be mopping up after Patrick's problems anymore. Lucas Kane appeared to be a big boy. If he was foolish enough to go blindly into a business deal with her brother, then he would have to pay the consequences. Teach him the restaurant business, indeed!

"What are you doing?" Kati demanded abruptly as Luke moved around the room picking up her kitchen supplies and tucking them under his arm.

"I'm leaving," he announced pleasantly, picking up a handful of wooden spoons and tucking them in the back pocket of his jeans. "Now which would you prefer, Kati, the top of the blender? Or the bottom? Personally it doesn't matter to me. Either is fine." He tried to hold back a smile at the look on her face.

"What do you mean, the top or the bottom? I want them both. Put that stuff down!" she demanded, moving across the room and yanking things out of his pocket. Ignoring her, Luke leisurely moved around the kitchen confiscating more items.

"What are you doing? Stop that!" Kati cried, grabbing his arm. She could feel every inch of his muscled forearm and despite her anger, a tingle licked up her skin. She snatched her hand free, absently wiping her palm on her apron.

"I'm leaving, just like you told me to, but you certainly can't expect me to leave without getting *something* for my investment?" One brow rose as his amusement increased. "Since I *do* own half this diner, plus two months' mortgage payments, it's only fair that half of the diner goes with me. I'm sure you'd agree. After all, you seem like a reasonable person, even if you are a bit cranky."

"Cranky!" Kati glowered at him. How dare he! "I am not cranky," she defended hotly, knowing all the while she was, but unable to help herself.

His dark brows grew together in concentrated thought. "Most of this stuff will be easy to move, but I don't know how I'm going to get half the stove out. Have you got any suggestions?" Smiling, Luke continued tucking things under his arms as he waited for her response.

"You can't—you can't—" Her eyes widened as he turned to look at her. "You can't possibly be serious!" Kati sputtered.

"Can't I?" His blue eyes danced as they fastened on hers. Kati held her breath as silence hung heavy in the air. Lord, what had Patrick done to her? He'd bartered his half of the diner to a madman!

"The way I see it, Kati," Luke continued, "I can either go, or I can stay. The choice is yours. But if I go, half the diner goes with me."

"That's blackmail!" she hissed fiercely, allowing her anger to boil over.

"One might look at it that way," Luke mused, his smile growing brighter. "But I prefer to think of it as protecting my investment."

Kati stared at him in annoyance, thoroughly confused. "Why? Why on earth would you, a man who admittedly knows nothing about a diner, insist on staying, especially when you know you're not wanted! I don't understand." Kati shook her head and Luke sighed. Somehow, he had the feeling that this wasn't the time to tell her that his money wasn't the only thing that suddenly was of interest to him.

"You don't have to understand, Kati," Luke said simply. "It won't be the first time I've not been wanted, but be that as it may, the choice is yours. I'm willing to stay and help out in any way I can. You just tell me what to do. If you want me to leave, I'll leave, but—" He waved his arm around the kitchen. Words weren't needed. Kati knew full well his intention. Her anger flamed in the face of reality, and a dash of sanity took over.

Kati paced the length of the room, trying to clear her cluttered thoughts. If this man did legally own half of her diner, well then, she hated to admit it, but maybe he did have a legal claim to half of everything in it. And right now, she couldn't afford to take the chance that he would up and walk off with her equipment. How on earth could she operate? She certainly didn't have the funds to start replacing things, not with the current state of her finances. No, that was simply not a viable option.

If keeping her diner, and keeping it *intact* meant letting Lucas Kane stay, well then, she'd just have to swallow her pride and let the blasted man stay! But if he thought for one moment she was going to help him or teach him anything, he had another guess coming. This was her diner, and while it may not have been much in other people's eyes, it was all she had. And she hadn't worked her fingers to the bone trying to keep it afloat so she could turn it over to the first man who walked through the door. It was hers, she thought fiercely. And hers alone. She didn't want to share it, she realized darkly. She wanted, deserved to own it all herself. But for now, she had no choice but to go along with him. At least until she could figure out something else to do.

"Mr. Kane, considering I have no choice in the matter," she stopped, spitting the words out like bullets, "you may stay." At Luke's relieved smile, she rushed on. "However, don't think for a moment that this is a permanent arrangement. I fully intend to have my attorneys check out that document." Kati failed to add that the only attorney in town was Wilfred Barnwood. Wilfred was nearing sixty, semiretired, and slightly hard of hearing. Of late, the only activity Wilfred engaged in was playing gin rummy in the park every afternoon. He was a wonderful caring man, but Kati wasn't certain he could deal with this kind of complicated legal matter. She, however, wasn't about to tell Lucas Kane that.

"By all means, please have anyone you like check it out." Luke set down his cache of equipment and pulled the wrinkled paper out of his back pocket. "I'm sure your attorneys will confirm this is a duly executed agreement." He grinned at her. "And please, call me Luke."

Kati snatched the paper out of his hand. Her fingers brushed his, and she tried to ignore the jolt of warmth that engulfed her.

"Kati?"

"What!" Kati refused to look at him, not liking the intensity of his blue eyes as they locked on hers. She pretended to be engrossed in the legal document, which she couldn't make heads or tails of.

"Something's burning," he said softly, pointing to the temperamental oven.

"Oh, no!" Kati whirled and yanked the oven door open. Smoke billowed through the kitchen as she pulled the second batch of burnt custard free. "If you want to be useful, Mr. Kane, then I suggest you start by fixing this oven. Since the diner is half yours, then half the problems are also yours. *It's only fair,*" she couldn't resist adding a bit smugly.

Kati dumped the second batch of custard into the garbage, cursing her brother, egg custard, and Lucas Kane all in one breath.

"Fix the oven?" came the tentative reply, and Kati bit back a smile. Being part owner of a diner might not be exactly what Lucas Kane envisioned. It just might be easier to get rid of the man than she thought.

"Yes, the oven. You know, this white piece of equipment that we bake in."

Luke frowned and bent down to glance cautiously at the smoking appliance. He was so close his husky male scent infiltrated her breathing space. Lord, he smelled sweeter than her maple syrup.

"What's, uh—what's wrong with it?" Luke asked, his eyes searching hers.

Kati dragged a hand through her hair, fearing she couldn't stop the smile that was threatening to break loose. If he could only see the look on his face. "If I knew what was wrong with it, I would have fixed it my-self."

Luke shifted uneasily. If she had asked him to tear down a wall, that he could do. But fix an oven? "But, uh, Kati, if we don't know what's wrong with it, how can we fix it?"

Kati smiled for the first time. "Not *we*. You. *You're* going to fix it. I don't care how. But I want this oven fixed." She paused deliberately for effect. "Tomorrow would be fine, Mr. Kane." She refused to use his first name. Keeping things on a more formal basis would make it easier for her to deal with him, easier to keep him at arm's length. There was something about the man that disturbed her, and it didn't have anything to do with his ownership papers, but more to do with the man himself.

"Tomorrow?" Luke echoed dully, scratching the back of his neck and hesitantly peering down at the oven again. For a fraction of an instant, Kati felt a twinge of remorse. It really wasn't fair to expect him to fix the oven. Admittedly he didn't know anything about running a diner.

On the other hand, she reminded herself, he *did* insist on full partnership rights, and with those rights came responsibilities as well. How he handled himself and the situation just might let her see what the man was made of. Remorse quickly vanished, replaced by a need to see if Lucas Kane was ready to back up his mouth with action. No doubt he would be gone quicker than her blueberry muffins on a Saturday morning when he realized he would actually have to work.

"Yes, Mr. Kane, tomorrow. Do whatever you have to, but tomorrow is Friday, and for six years Fridays have been perch and baked macaroni day. I certainly can't bake macaroni or much else if the oven isn't fixed, now can I?" She couldn't help the grin that spread across her lips as Luke let loose a low whistle.

One brow rose pleadingly. "Tomorrow?"

Kati nodded her head. "And since it's almost four," she said, tapping her watch for effect, "I suggest you get cracking."

Luke simply stood there for a moment, scratching his head and glancing from her to the oven. The air crackled with electricity, but Kati refused to back down. If things worked out as she expected, by this time tomorrow Lucas Kane would only be a bad blemish on her memory.

"Do you have a tape measure?" Luke asked suddenly, his face brightening.

Taken aback by his strange request, Kati frowned at him. A tape measure? He was going to fix her oven with a tape measure? This man apparently didn't have both his oars in the water. But what did she expect from one of Patrick's friends?

When she didn't answer him, Luke turned, yanked open a drawer and began to rifle through it. Sighing in exasperation, Kati reached out and slammed the drawer shut, nearly catching his fingers.

"Mr. Kane." Exasperated, she drew the words out slowly. "I know you don't know anything about running a diner, or repairing an oven, but I can tell you from first-hand experience, a tape measure is hardly the tool you'll need.''

Luke leaned his hip against the counter and looked at her carefully. ''You said you didn't care how I fixed the oven, so let me do it my way. Just this once, all right?'' His engaging smile only made her more wary.

Resentment tightened her body and Kati boldly met his gaze, swallowing nervously as a wild tingle warmed her body. Instinctively she took a step back, wanting nothing more than to put some distance between her and Lucas Kane. She never thought of the kitchen as particularly small, but with this man in it, it seemed miniature.

''Just this once?'' he prodded softly, reaching out to brush a wayward strand of hair from her face. His touch caused her nerves to squawk in silent alarm.

''All right!'' She fumed taking another step back. ''Do it your way. Just remember what I said,'' she threatened, ignoring the amusement dancing in his eyes. ''I want the oven fixed by tomorrow.''

''Aye, aye, chief.'' Luke gave Kati a mock salute as she turned on her heel and stormed through the swinging door. Scratching his chin absently, Luke stared long and hard after her. She was beautiful, but Lord, that disposition of hers!

A thought suddenly occurred to him and he threw back his head and laughed. No wonder she was being so churlish. How would he feel if some stranger suddenly showed up and announced he was part owner of Kane Construction? A reluctant smile tugged at his mouth. No one would have the nerve. Well, he mused, on second thought, maybe Kati Rose Ryan would. Somehow, he had to convince her that he wasn't going to harm her or her diner. He might even be able to help. And from the looks of this place, she could use some help.

"You're not going to get very much done, standing there grinning and daydreaming," Kati scolded as she walked back into the kitchen carrying a tray full of salads.

"Here, let me help you." Luke reached out and tried to take the tray from her hands.

"I don't need your help," she hissed, holding on to the plastic tray for dear life and resenting his presence. Help her, indeed! "I'm quite capable of handling things on my own," she said pointedly, giving the tray a good tug to release his hold. The force of her jerky movement caused the salad bowls to slide precariously to one side. Luke reached out, and his big hands quickly grabbed the tray, steadying it.

Kati lifted her embarrassed eyes to his and felt a hot flush creep slowly up her face. Maybe he was only trying to be polite, but if he weren't underfoot and in her way this wouldn't have happened in the first place. Swallowing hard, she averted her gaze. When he looked at her with those eyes, she felt so—so—twitchy.

"Thank you," she said finally, because it was the only polite thing to do. "I—I—I—do you think you could get out of my kitchen now?" If she ever hoped to get any work done this afternoon, she had to get him out of her way, and out of her vision. He was definitely a distraction. She needed some time alone, some time to think. And she couldn't very well do it with him watching her every move.

"I'll be out front if you need me." Luke crossed the kitchen, letting the door swing shut softly behind him.

"Need you!" Kati snorted in disgust at Luke's retreating back as she slammed the tray of salads down. What would she need *him* for?

How could Patrick do this to her? Kati wondered dismally as her eyes pooled with tears again. Her brother had destroyed her nice, safe world in one foolish, foolish move. Why on earth would he put up the diner as collateral on a loan? And why on earth would Lucas Kane give him one? Kane might be handsome, but he obviously wasn't too bright. Giving Patrick money was like giving a thief the keys to the vault. Lifting her apron, Kati dashed at her damp face.

She had no doubt Lucas Kane was telling her the truth. But now, the problem was how to get rid of him. The last thing in the world she needed was another partner. Patrick, her own flesh and blood, was bad enough, but a stranger who knew nothing about the business—well, that was asking too much even of her!

This diner was hers, and hers alone! she thought fiercely. She was the one who worked it six days a week, making sure everything ran smoothly. And she wasn't about to let some stranger, no matter how attractive, come in and start interfering! She had to find a way to get rid of him!

"Kati? You all right?" Bessie peeked around the door, her brows furrowed in concern. Bessie was Kati's self-appointed guardian and stuck her nose everywhere, whether it belonged or not. But Kati loved the woman dearly.

Kati forced a smile. No sense worrying Bessie. "I'm fine. Just trying to figure out what I'm going to do."

"Do? What's to do? Seems to me you'd welcome some help around here. That Kane fellow can't be any worse than Patrick. Your brother never did do anything around here but cost you money."

"Bessie!" Kati was shocked, never expecting Bessie to take Lucas Kane's side. "What on earth am I going to do with another partner? One who doesn't know the first thing about the business, yet?''

"As it stands right now, Kane's already pulled his weight by paying the back mortgage. At least we don't have to worry about being evicted. Seems to me that's something to be grateful for.'' Bessie sniffed. "Just saw him out front, says he's going to see about fixing the oven. Maybe his coming is a blessing in disguise.''

A shudder of rage raced through Kati. "A blessing? The man thinks he's going to fix my oven with a tape measure, and Bessie, have you forgotten my brother's other friends? The first one stole four hundred dollars from—''

Bessie raised her hand in the air. "Honey, this Kane fellow seems different somehow. Sure is a handsome one, and Kati, he genuinely seems to want to help. Why don't you give him a chance?''

"Handsome!'' Kati snorted in disgust, refusing to admit that she indeed found Lucas Kane handsome. And attractive. "What has that got to do with anything? As to giving him a chance—for what? So he can steal from me, or take my diner away?'' Kati shook her head furiously, fighting back tears again. "Not a chance, Bessie. He may be part owner of this diner, but not because I want or need him. He's the last thing I need right now. The sooner I can get rid of him, the better.''

"Ladies?'' Mr. Tibbits' voice floated through the screen door and all thoughts of Lucas Kane and the problems she was facing fled for the moment as Kati turned to face the portly man. When it rained, it poured, she thought, swallowing back a curse and forcing her lips into a polite, if tight smile. The Kaline County health inspector gave her the willies. He was always patting her, or brushing against her, or looking at her in a way she found strangely offensive. She always had the feeling he was more interested in inspecting her, rather than the diner.

He hadn't actually done anything, at least not anything that Kati could complain to his supervisors about, but just his mere presence was enough to set her nerves on edge. As if they weren't on edge enough today.

"How nice to see you both," he purred softly, "particularly *you*, Kati Rose. May I come in?" Kati and Bessie exchanged glances. As much as she wanted to, Kati couldn't very well tell him he *couldn't* come in. As the owner of a restaurant, she was subject to unannounced inspections from the county health department whenever they so desired. It just seemed like ever since Tibbits took over this territory, she'd had an inordinate number of inspections.

He opened the door and attempted to enter, but Kati put her arm out, blocking his path. "I'm sorry, Mr. Tibbits," she said firmly. "You know I don't allow smoking in my kitchen." It had been a running battle between them. The smell from his cigar lingered in the air for hours, permeating her food, and no matter how she tried she couldn't get rid of the stench. She always suffered from a pounding headache after one of his visits, but she wasn't sure if it was from the cigar, or the man himself.

Mr. Tibbits' beady eyes narrowed as he clamped his lips firmly around the slimy stub of his cigar. His eyes wandered a leisurely path over her. Kati grew increasingly uncomfortable when she realized where his eyes were staring. She deliberately crossed her arms over her chest.

Taking one final puff, he tossed the cigar to the ground, stepped on it, and sauntered into the kitchen.

"Want me to stay?" Bessie asked, frowning at the man as he slowly walked around the room.

"No, that won't be necessary," Mr. Tibbits answered before Kati could open her mouth. "I just have a few things to discuss with Kati." His mouth curved upward again. "Privately."

Not liking either his tone or his words, Kati straightened her spine. "Mr. Tibbits," she said, trying to keep a firm grip on her growing temper. "I believe my employee was speaking to me. Unless you have some health objection, *I* would prefer to give my staff directives."

"Sorry," he said smartly, giving her an apologetic wave. Kati decided not to let the man get to her.

"Bessie, it's been pretty quiet in here all afternoon, but it's almost the dinner rush and I'm sure we're going to start getting busy. Why don't you go on out front?"

Bessie hesitated, looking from the man to Kati. "Go on," Kati urged with a smile. "Everything will be fine."

Giving the man a none too pleasant look, Bessie turned on her heel and pushed through the door, muttering softly under her breath.

"Now," Kati said firmly, annoyed at yet another irritation in an already irritating day. She crossed the room to stand a good distance away from the man. "What is it that you wanted?"

Cocking his head to one side, he smiled crookedly. The look on his face caused a flash of fear to rock her.

"You," he said simply.

Chapter Three

Kati blinked, not wanting to believe what her ears had heard. "I beg your pardon?"

Mr. Tibbits inched closer to her. A skitter of alarm skated up Kati's spine, but she quickly dismissed it. She was overreacting, she chided herself, backing up against the counter.

Mr. Tibbits was a perfectly harmless, middle-aged man, with a generous middle, an unpleasant personality, and a faint odor about him that no amount of cologne could erase. That certainly didn't mean he was going to harm her, did it? Perhaps because of all the confusion today she had misunderstood him. She had been overreacting all day, she realized belatedly.

"I see you haven't gotten that oven fixed yet, Kati," he said softly.

"Tomorrow," she stammered, ducking around him. "The oven will be fixed tomorrow."

"That's what your waitress told me the last time I was here." He moved up behind her until she could feel the heat of his breath on her neck.

"It really will be fixed tomorrow," she insisted, praying her voice wasn't trembling nearly as badly as her insides were, while moving out of his range again. "I've—I've spoken to someone about it today and they've assured me that it will be fixed tomorrow." Lucas Kane better make good on his promise, she thought darkly.

"I could write you up for it, Kati." He moved in behind her. He was so close his words danced off her neck. Gritting her teeth, Kati inched away from him. She would not beg, she told herself firmly. If he wanted to write her up about the oven, then let him. If he wanted to fine her, or close her down, so be it! She would not stoop to begging. Not to anyone. Not for anything.

"Word has it that you've been letting animals in your diner. County takes a dim view of that, Kati." If he was deliberately trying to egg her on, he was doing a good job of it. Her temper flared and she whirled to face him, cursing Mr. Billings, Beauregard, and Vera, who no doubt had reported her.

"For your information Mr. Tibbits," she snapped haughtily, "animals are allowed in the finest establishments in Europe."

"Perhaps," he said slowly, his voice cold and unfriendly. "But this ain't Europe. Something like that, well, I might have to close you up for good. For the good of the public's health, of course." His thin lips parted in a smug grin.

Of course, she thought dully, staring at him and trying to figure out what was going on. He was after something, it was as clear as the mole on his face. "What do you want?" she demanded, feigning bravery.

"Well, I suppose I could be persuaded to overlook these offenses. Not that they're minor, mind you. They'd sure take a lot of overlooking."

Resisting the urge to slap the smug look off his face, Kati finally realized what he wanted. "Mr. Tibbits," she said coldly, looking him square in the eye. "If it's money you're after, you're out of luck. I don't have any." There, now that he knew she wasn't about to offer him a bribe, maybe he'd leave her alone.

He slowly licked his lips. "There are other things besides money in this world, Kati Rose." His eyes went over her again and a sinking feeling began to spread through her limbs. It suddenly hit her what he was after. If she was a man, she'd deck him! How dare he!

She'd play dumb, she decided, at least until she could think of something better to do under the circumstances.

"What other things?" she asked, frowning. "I'd be happy to send some food home with you for your family if you like." Even to her own ears she couldn't believe how ridiculous that sounded.

His steady gaze made her pulse quicken in alarm. "Food's not quite what I had in mind."

Her temper quickly overruled her tongue. "And just what exactly did you have in mind?" One brow rose as she dared him to answer.

He lifted his hand, running his fingers slowly down her bare arm. "Well, let's just say what I had in mind is a bit more personal."

Enough playing cat and mouse with this creep. She was going to make him say it out loud. And when he did— "How personal?" she demanded. "Could you be more specific?"

"I think what the man had in mind was you served up on a gleaming platter." Luke was standing in the doorway, and from the look on his face, Kati knew he had heard most, if not all of the conversation. A heated rush suffused her cheeks at being caught in such a position. "Is that about right?" Luke asked softly. A rush of fierce protectiveness rose up in him, catching him unaware. Seeing this man paw Kati, all his instincts leaped to life.

She tried not to show the relief she felt at his sudden presence. She didn't need him, she assured herself. She was perfectly capable of handling things on her own, without Lucas Kane sticking his crooked nose where it didn't belong.

Mr. Tibbits dropped his hand from Kati's arm and looked at Luke suspiciously. "And who might you be, son?"

Luke crossed the room, wedging himself between Kati and the inspector. Kati glared at Luke's broad back. Arrogant, interfering man. Why didn't he just go away and leave her to her business? She was perfectly capable of handling Tibbits, and anything else that happened to come her way. Did she look like she needed a bodyguard?

"I'm not your son," Luke said slowly, his voice tight. "And the name's Kane. Lucas Kane." His words were low, his tone deep. Tight control echoed on each and every syllable as his voice boomed around the tension-filled room. Instinctively Kati knew that if Lucas Kane ever lost his temper, it wouldn't be a pretty sight.

Tibbits' lips tightened and he looked around Luke to her. "Kati Rose, perhaps you ought to tell this young man who I am."

"His name is Tibbits," she announced, tugging on Luke's arm until he tilted his head to look at her. "He's the county health inspector," she whispered frantically, clutching Luke's sleeve. "And he *can* close me down, so would you mind staying out of this?"

Tibbits' eyes glinted smugly as he shoved a cigar in his mouth and lit it. Ignoring her, Luke promptly yanked the cigar loose from the man's lips. "You're a health inspector," Luke scolded, dropping the cigar to the ground and stomping on it with his booted foot. "You should know smoking is bad for your health."

Kati groaned inwardly. Hell's bells! Now Luke had really done it. She had no doubt Tibbits was going to write her up and close her down. Pronto. Why hadn't Luke left well enough alone? She could have strangled him! Why must the man interfere in things that didn't concern him?

Tibbits' face grew livid. "Young man," he said menacingly, pointing his finger in Luke's face. "You'll be sorry for that. One word, that's all it will take to close this place down."

"Jamison," Luke said softly, looking as if he was deep in thought. "Is Ralph Jamison still head of the County Health Department?" Confused, Kati tried to peer over Luke's shoulder to see what was going on, but Luke was just too darn tall, so she gave him a poke in the back just to remind him she was still there. The man had suddenly taken charge, and he didn't even know what he'd taken charge of! And she deeply resented it.

"You know Jamison?" Tibbits inquired in a suddenly small voice. His face paled noticeably.

Luke rocked back on his heels and crossed his arms over his broad chest. "Sure do. We go way back. Tell me, Tibbits, how do you think Ralph will feel when he learns that you're using sexual harassment on the business owners of this county? The *female* business owners?"

Tibbits snatched a faded hanky from his back pocket and began to mop his brow. "I—I—uhm, I'm sure you've got this all wrong, Mr. Kane." He mopped his brow faster. "I surely didn't intend to give you the impression I was trying to—that I was—" He stopped abruptly and glanced at Kati who glowered at him.

Lying weasel, she thought disgustedly. He wasn't even man enough to admit what he had done.

"Kati, do you think we've misjudged this man's intention?" Luke asked, turning to flash her a quick smile. She had to admit, the man had a glorious smile.

"I'm not really sure." She frowned. Let Tibbits sweat for a while, she thought vengefully. Maybe he'd think twice about trying this with some other woman business owner who was at his mercy.

"Really, Kati Rose," Tibbits gushed, his voice pleading. "I truly am sorry if I gave you the impression I was trying to... well... you know."

"Yes," she said firmly, looking him square in the eye. "I do know. Now I want you to know. If you ever try anything like that again, I won't be responsible for my actions."

Tibbits nodded his head furiously. Obviously he had gotten her message.

"Nor will I," Luke told Tibbits, clamping his large calloused hand down solidly on the other man's shoulder. "And believe me, I don't make promises I can't keep." Luke's meaning was clear, his words hanging heavy in the silent room.

Shifting uncomfortably from foot to foot, Tibbits waited for Luke to release his shoulder. "I'm sorry about the misunderstanding, Kati Rose," he said softly, mopping a line of perspiration off his upper lip. "Now that I know things are in order," he paused to cast a glance at

Luke. "I probably won't have to be coming around so often."

"What a shame," Kati said sarcastically, her anger and resentment at the man still intact.

"Well, I really must be going. Make sure you get that oven fixed, now." Tibbits stuck out his hand to Luke who blatantly ignored it. "Good day." Tibbits hustled himself to the door, turning back now and again just to make sure Luke wasn't following on his heels.

Heaving a sigh of relief, Kati whirled on Luke, fire dancing in her eyes. "What the hell did you do that for?" she demanded. "I'm perfectly capable of handling things on my own. Do I look like I need a keeper?"

"As a matter of fact, it might not be a bad idea," Luke told her with a wicked smile. "You didn't seem to be handling things too well when I walked in," he reminded her, and she flushed. He was right. If he hadn't come in just when he did, she didn't know what she would have done, short of bopping Tibbits over the head with a pan, which was certainly no solution.

She just wasn't used to having other people take care of things for her. She was used to doing everything—for everybody. Why had she allowed Luke to take over the situation? She wished she knew. The fact of the matter was he had, and she was just a bit resentful. She had a feeling Lucas Kane was the kind of man who was used to being in charge, used to having his orders carried out. But this was her diner. Hers, she thought fiercely! And she wasn't about to start taking orders from him, papers or no papers!

Still, she thought grudgingly, he had gotten her out of a potentially ugly situation, and she probably should thank him. It really was the only polite thing to do, under the circumstances.

"Luke," she said, forcing herself to be polite and hating it all the while. "I want to thank you for handling Tibbits." Deliberately she averted her gaze. Looking directly into Luke's eyes was just too disconcerting for her shattered nervous system. At least for the moment. "I must admit I was very fortunate to have you come along just when you did, not to mention the fact that you happened to know Tibbits' boss. What was his name?"

"Jamison—and I don't know the man. As a matter of fact, we've never met. I wouldn't know him if he danced naked right here in this room."

Kati almost choked. "What? What do you mean you don't know the man? But, I thought you told—you said—" Luke held up his hand.

"I know what I said. I know Ralph Jamison's name, but nothing else about him except the fact that he's head of the Public Health Department for Libertyville." He shrugged nonchalantly. "That's all there is to it. It was just lucky, I guess."

"Do you mean to tell me you bluffed Tibbits?" Her voice was incredulous.

A loud booming laugh erupted from Luke's chest, and Kati's temper flared. She certainly didn't see what was so funny, particularly when it was her business that had been at stake. What if Tibbits had called Luke's bluff!

"I really don't see what's so funny. I could have lost everything because of you!" she huffed.

"*We*," he corrected gently. "We could have lost everything and Kati, I never would have lost the bluff. I deal a great poker hand." Luke looked at her, his expression serious. "I think we should talk," he said abruptly and Kati ran her damp palms down her apron and averted her gaze.

"What's to talk about?" Anxious to avoid any more confrontations, she turned and moved around the kitchen in a flurry of activity. She could handle this man when he was the enemy, but when he was on her side, she wasn't so sure. She had to keep moving, keep thinking.

Luke clamped his hand down on her shoulders, halting her movements. "Kati," he said gently turning her around to face him. "You move faster than a Kansas City twister. Now stand still and look at me." He lifted a hand to tilt her chin upward. "I think we got off on the wrong foot," he admitted with a lopsided smile that softened her resentment. "I'm not going to hurt you," he said softly, running his thumb along the delicate skin of her jaw.

Kati blinked. "Then why are you here?"

"I already told you, Kati. I'm your new partner."

"I don't want a partner," she said glumly, lowering her gaze to study one of the buttons on his shirt. It wasn't going to be so easy to get rid of him, she realized belatedly.

"Tough," Luke said, stroking her chin gently.

"But I already have a partner," she protested, feeling ridiculous because she was now talking to the man's broad chest. And enjoying it. "I can tell you from experience that it won't work."

"It will," he said firmly. "You may have had a partner before, but—"

"There's no buts about it, Mr. Kane. I don't want or need another partner. I can handle things perfectly fine on my own, without your help."

"No, you can't," he said, and her angry gaze flew upward. The look in his eyes caused her pulse to play hopscotch.

"Oh, can't I?" she snapped, her eyes blazing in challenge.

Luke sighed heavily, his massive shoulders moving against the fabric of his shirt. "Face facts, Kati, you're running this place single-handedly, but the truth of the matter is, *you're not running it, it's running you.* You're behind on your mortgage payments, you've got an oven that doesn't do much except belch smoke, you've got inspectors crawling all over the place—" Luke stopped abruptly as she blinked back tears.

"Kati?" Luke's voice caressed her, washing over her with a heated warmth. "I know you don't like the idea of having me around, but if you'll just give me a chance, you'll see I can be helpful." It suddenly meant a great deal to him to have her believe him. Neither Patrick nor his lost money seemed as important as having this woman's trust. He had a feeling she didn't give it easily, or often, and for some reason it made it all the more important to him.

Kati glared at him. "Mr. Kane, the last time I allowed one of my brother's so-called *friends* to be helpful, he helped himself to four hundred of *my* dollars. That's why I'm behind in the mortgage payment, and why the oven's not fixed yet! Not because I'm as incompetent as you've so graciously suggested!" She didn't know why, but the idea that Luke thought she was a blundering idiot annoyed her. She wanted him to know that the reason everything was going to pot was because she had trusted another one of her brother's friends. She was not about to make the same mistake again. Particularly with this man. Especially with this man!

Luke looked at her incredulously. "You think I'm going to steal from you?"

"I don't know what you're going to do," she defended hotly, dragging a hand through her hair.

"I hate to be blunt, Kati, but you really don't have much worth stealing. A broken-down oven is hardly what I'd call a marketable commodity." Luke pulled a clean handkerchief from his pocket and dabbed at the moisture on her cheeks. The gesture was so sudden and unexpected, Kati looked up at him, trying to ignore the tenderness in his eyes. "Give me a chance, Kati, that's all I ask. Just a chance. Under the circumstances, I really don't think you have any choice. I do own half of this place," he reminded her.

As if she could forget! She studied his face, looking for some clue, some hint as to why he was doing this. Why on earth would he want to be part owner of a diner?

"Why?" she asked abruptly. "Why do you want to stay?"

Luke shrugged his shoulders. "I want to help. And why shouldn't I? I have a vested interest in this place. If the situation was reversed, wouldn't you expect to stay?"

She stared doubtfully at him for a moment. He had a point, she realized darkly. It wasn't his fault that Patrick had sold him a bill of goods. How could she just throw him out on the street? He *did* own half the diner, so how could she simply dismiss him just because she didn't want him there? She couldn't. She may be a lot of things, but unfair or unjust she wasn't. Lucas Kane had just as much right to stay and work the diner as she did. All the man wanted was a chance.

Like it or not, she was going to have to let him stay. But she wasn't about to make it easy on him. If he really wanted to be a partner, he was going to have to work. She was tired of carrying everyone. Lucas Kane would have to pull his weight, or she would send him packing. But as long as he was here, she might as well make the best of the situation.

Pretending to weigh her options, Kati finally nodded. "All right," she agreed, her voice none too happy. "But I'm warning you, you pull your own weight, do what you're told and stay out of trouble. Understand?"

"Kati." Laughing softly, Luke dropped his hands to her shoulders and gave her a little shake. "I'm your *partner*. You don't have to give me orders."

Kati blinked up at him as his words echoed through her head. She had never dealt with a man, *any* man who could hold his own and pull his weight. It wasn't going to be easy, but she at least had to try. It was the only thing to do under the circumstances.

"Luke...I'm—I'm sorry. I'm not usually so—so—" Kati searched for a word adequate enough to describe her behavior.

"So rude?" Luke offered helpfully.

Kati nodded and flushed.

"And cantankerous?"

She nodded again, growing redder.

"Crotchety and bad-tempered?" His husky voice was filled with humor and Kati couldn't help but smile. Under the circumstances he was being very kind. She wasn't so sure she could have been as generous if the situations were reversed.

"You left out ill-mannered," she told him, sighing. Her strength and resistance defused, Kati rested her forehead against his broad chest, feeling like an idiot for all the things she had said and done to him since he had walked into the diner.

"I was getting to that," he said softly, lifting a hand to stroke the back of her hair. Just for a moment, she allowed herself the pleasure of his comfort.

"You know what your problem is?" he asked, and her head snapped up.

Five minutes and already he was going to tell her what her problems were! What did she expect from a friend of her brother? Her defenses instantly went up.

"No," she snapped, feeling unaccountably threatened, "but I have a feeling you're about to tell me!"

"Your problem is you're used to dealing with little boys who pretend to be men." His voice dropped to a husky whisper that caused her pulse to dance deliriously. "I'm not your little brother, Kati. I'm a man."

"A man," she repeated dully. The word echoed through her mind and she couldn't help but wonder how on earth such a harmless word could suddenly sound so ominous.

"Yes, Kati," he said huskily. "A man." The big callused hands that had so gently stroked her hair now slipped around her waist, pulling her closer. Kati's breathing slowed, and her thoughts tangled like thread on a spindle as he gathered her reluctant body close.

Suddenly wary, Kati stiffened as the heat of his body warmed hers. Maybe she couldn't do anything about this partnership business, but she sure could do something about this physical attraction that arced between them.

"Please?" she whispered, her eyes pleading. She raised a hand to his chest to put some distance between them, but the rapid beat of his heart beneath his shirt frightened her beyond measure. It matched the rate of hers.

"Please what?" Luke was so close, his sweet breath beat upon her skin until she was certain he could see her quivering. "Did you know you smelled good?" he whispered, burying his face in her luxuriant hair. She wiggled uncomfortably.

"Do the women you know smell bad?" Kati asked flippantly, wanting only to break the thread that seemed to be tugging her closer to him.

"Oh, Kati." A deep masculine chuckle broke loose from his chest. Tightening his arms around her, Luke brought his mouth ever so close to hers.

She tried to take a deep breath, but somehow she couldn't, the air seemed to jostle her rib cage. Instinctively, she licked her lips, knowing he was going to kiss her, yet feeling powerless to stop him. Her eyes met his. Knots tightened her stomach and she felt like she'd been stuck in a vise. There was something in his eyes, something she couldn't identify, but she knew it frightened her.

"Kati." His words came out a soft moan and her lips fell open in breathless anticipation as she raised her face to his.

It was wrong, her mind screamed, but her body and her senses paid no heed. Guilt and fear evaporated like fog on a misty morning as Luke's lips gently lowered over hers.

The first touch of his mouth was brief and light, like a ray of sun glancing off the first spring flower. Her eyes jerked open in stunned disbelief as his touch jolted through her, weakening her limbs and stunning her already dazed senses.

Sensing her fear, Luke's lips slowly caressed her, drawing and coaxing a response until her lashes lowered again and she sighed, not knowing if it was desire or despair that rocked her.

Shyly, she kissed him back, letting her own lips follow the movement of his. Luke coiled his fingers through her silky mass of curls, pulling her closer. She slid her arms around him, enjoying the masculine feel of him. He was all muscle and hardness, and she allowed her senses the full pleasure of him as her hands caressed his broad back, his wide shoulders.

Expertly his mouth explored hers, demanding a response her traitorous body gave. Tantalizing shock waves rippled through her, leaving burning desire in their wake. She drank in his sweetness, knowing she was growing more intoxicated with each nerve-splitting second.

Luke sighed against her mouth, his breathing shallow and ragged. Lifting his head, his blue eyes settled on her swollen lips and a flush crept up her face.

"A *man*, Kati," he said firmly, tapping the end of her nose affectionately. "Try not to forget it."

Astonishment widened her eyes as Luke turned and walked from the kitchen. As if in a trance, Kati lifted a hand to touch her swollen lips, feeling an unexpected quickening in her pulse. A *man*, her mind echoed, and she shook her head. How on earth could she forget? But more importantly, how on earth was she going to get rid of him?

Chapter Four

W here is he?'' Kati demanded the next morning as she
yanked open the screen door to the diner.

"Who?" Bessie rounded the counter to pour fresh
coffee for Vera. Vera's ears perked up at the sight of Kati.

"My partner," Kati hissed, making the word sound as
angry as she felt.

"Luke?" Bessie frowned. "Honey, he's out back in
the kitchen. Why?" Her eyes narrowed suspiciously.
"What's got you so riled up this morning, Kati Rose?"

"At four o'clock this morning I heard—" Kati stopped
abruptly. Vera was leaning out of the booth in an effort
to hear and was in imminent danger of falling flat on her
well-made-up face. Grabbing Bessie by the arm, Kati
steered her into a corner and deliberately lowered her
voice. "I don't know what Luke was doing in my diner
in the middle of the night, but I heard the most ungodly
noises coming from down here. Doesn't the man know I

live right upstairs?'' she hissed. "I don't know what he was doing in my diner at that hour, but if he thinks—''

"Kati, wait—he's wasn't doing—Luke didn't—'' Bessie stopped abruptly at Kati's scowl.

"Don't tell me *you're* going to start sticking up for him?'' Kati demanded, one brow arching in surprise.

"Kati Rose Ryan!'' Bessie huffed indignantly. "I'm not sticking up for anyone. But before you go getting yourself all worked up, you'd better go see just what the man's been doing!''

"I can just imagine what he's been doing,'' Kati muttered, turning and storming across the diner with Bessie right on her heels.

"Luke?'' Kati called, pushing through the swinging door and stopping so abruptly Bessie bumped into her. "Luke! Where are you?''

"Right here,'' Luke said from somewhere inside the refrigerator. All she could see was a pair of long jean-clad legs and a rather large pair of feet.

"What are you doing in *my* refrigerator?'' Kati demanded, resisting the urge to rush over and slam the refrigerator door shut, preferably with him in it! The sight of someone, particularly *him* in her kitchen first thing in the morning immediately set her off. All her protective instincts rose to the surface. This was her private domain, and she wasn't accustomed to finding someone in here nosing around.

"Oh Lordy,'' Bessie muttered, shaking her head and rolling her eyes toward the heavens.

"*Your* kitchen?'' Luke said mildly, pulling his head out to look at her. "I thought we settled all this last night.'' One dark brow lifted in mild censure and Kati silently cursed her quick tongue.

"Sorry," she said, forcing herself to be polite. "Poor choice of words. By the way, what *are* you doing?"

"Just rearranging some supplies." Luke closed the refrigerator door, and Kati tried not to grind her teeth. For a man who didn't know anything about the restaurant business, he certainly seemed right at home. The man apparently hadn't wasted any time trying to take over!

Glaring at him, she noted absently that he was dressed much the same as yesterday. A pair of faded jeans clung to his lean hips and long legs. His shirt today was brown plaid, complemented with pearl snap buttons left open at the collar. Kati tried to ignore the flash of bare bronzed skin and dark curly hair that peeked through the opening. She was not about to be sidetracked by a handsome face or a beautiful pair of baby blue eyes.

"You look pretty worked up this morning, Kati," Luke teased, his eyes dancing wickedly. "What's the matter, Karma out of whack again?"

His words caused her temper to flare. Clenching her fists at her side, Kati took a threatening step closer, fully intending to throw him out bodily, if need be. Patience, she cautioned herself, coming to an abrupt halt. She couldn't let him get to her. Once Luke got wind of the kind of work involved in the day-to-day running of a diner, she had no doubt he would bolt as fast as his long legs could carry him. Until then, she had to control her temper and her tongue. But that didn't prevent her mind from imagining all the things she'd like to do to him.

"I want to know what you were doing in *my*—" Kati inhaled slowly, trying to calm herself "—in the diner in the middle of the night, making enough racket to raise the dead!" Inching closer until she was practically toe to toe with the man, Kati looked up into his amused face, not certain if the rapid thump of her pulse was from her anger or from the man's nearness. "Did you think I wouldn't hear you?" she asked incredulously. "I live right upstairs!"

"Now, Kati Rose," Bessie soothed. "It's not his fault. Luke here didn't know you lived upstairs and besides..." Her voice trailed off as Kati slowly turned and fixed her with a glare.

"What were you doing?" Kati asked him again.

"Just what you told me to do," Luke said with a lazy smile. He leaned his hip against the counter and poured himself a cup of coffee.

"What *I* told you to do?" Kati's eyes narrowed suspiciously, wondering what kind of game he was playing. "The only thing I told you to do was *leave*. And I don't recall that you paid much attention. *You're still here*," she couldn't help adding.

Luke drained his cup and set it down on the counter. He reached out, dropped his hands to her shoulders and spun her around before she could open her mouth to protest. Kati's eyes widened and a soft whimper escaped her lips. A brand new commercial stove with the latest up-to-date features sat proudly in the corner.

"Oh, my word!" Kati breathed softly, letting her eyes caress the new appliance. When she told him to fix the stove she had no idea the man would go out and buy her a new one! Blinking away her shock, Kati turned to him, her brows furrowed in confusion. "But how—when—I don't understand."

"Told you so," Bessie gloated, sliding her hands in the pockets of her apron and smiling smugly.

"What happened to the old stove?" Kati asked, shaking her head in confusion. This was totally unexpected, and left her feeling slightly off balance.

"You told me yesterday you wanted the stove fixed by today," Luke said calmly. "Now we both know that my knowledge of the restaurant business isn't exactly extensive. But I do know when an appliance is beyond repair." He shrugged. "Yesterday I ordered the new stove. I was going to tell you, but when I came in here yesterday afternoon you had your hands full with Tibbits. And after Tibbits left, well... His eyes gleamed wickedly and Kati shifted her frame. Did he have to remind her about the kiss they shared? She'd been trying hard to forget it!

Flustered now, Kati turned her gaze to the new stove. Her gratefulness was all mixed up with her fear. What business did he have buying her a new stove? she wondered crossly. Even if he did own half the diner, he had no right. He hadn't even asked her! She didn't want, nor would she accept any help from this man. Not money, not labor and most especially not his kindness!

This was her diner, Kati thought fiercely. *Hers!* She'd learned the hard way never to depend on anyone but herself, and that wasn't about to change now, partner or no partner! She didn't need him, or his newfangled appliances! Resentment burned deep, coiling her nerves as tight as a rope.

"How did you get it in here?" Kati asked suddenly, watching Bessie and Luke exchange furtive glances. Why did she get the feeling that something was going on here, and she was going to be the last one to know? Kati glanced from one to the other and they both grinned.

"I gave him my key," Bessie finally announced and Kati's eyes widened in stunned disbelief.

"You what?" Bessie, her loyal devoted employee, had apparently crossed over to the enemy! What kind of spell had Lucas Kane cast over the usually cautious woman?

Kati wondered. Probably the same charming one he had cast over her last night, Kati mused, trying not to smile.

"How'd you expect him to get the stove in," Bessie inquired, as if daring Kati to object, "through the window?"

That was just the point, Kati thought in panic. She didn't want Lucas Kane in here, she wanted him *out*! The sooner the better.

"Don't you have some work to do?" Kati asked Bessie pointedly, giving her the eye.

"Don't need no building to fall on me to let me know I'm not wanted," Bessie huffed, pushing through the swinging door.

Feeling Luke's eyes on her, Kati quickly turned away. The way he was looking at her dragged up a longing from somewhere deep inside, and she found herself slightly breathless. Perhaps she shouldn't have been so quick to send Bessie out front. She wasn't certain she wanted to be alone with this man, wasn't sure she trusted herself to be alone with him.

"We had a heck of a time getting the stove through the door," Luke explained, rubbing his chin absently. "It took longer than I expected, so I made breakfast for the deliverymen. Don't worry, I paid for the food. If you'll check the register you'll see the money's in there."

"I wasn't concerned about the money for the food," she said lamely, feeling a sudden bout of shame for her behavior. She knew he was standing right behind her and the urge to bolt grew strong. "Must have cost a fortune," she murmured, struggling to keep the conversation going and on a professional level. When there was no answer forthcoming, Kati tilted her head a bit until his face came into view. Her eyes slid over his features, and she felt herself inexplicably drawn to him. Lord, he was handsome!

"Did it?" Kati finally stammered, finding her voice.

"Depends on what your idea of a fortune is." His eyes snared hers as he propelled her around by the shoulders. Kati squirmed uncomfortably as the warmth of his hands seeped through the thin cotton of her blouse, sending her heart thumping into overtime. How could his eyes be so blue, she wondered, knowing it would be much easier to keep this man at bay if he wasn't so darn good-looking and good-natured. Why couldn't the man have three chins, and a big ol' black wart? she wondered miserably. Certainly then, well, she amended mentally, *maybe* then she'd be able to keep her wits about her. Kati had a feeling nothing could detract from this man's virility. It throbbed from every inch of him.

"You're not going to say it, are you?" Luke asked, his eyes glinting in humor.

"Say what?" she inquired, trying to pretend that his nearness wasn't affecting her.

"That you were wrong about me." A lopsided grin spread across his face, and she caught a flash of perfectly white teeth.

"Wrong!" She had no idea her face was as transparent as a bride's nighty!

"Yes, wrong. And that you're sorry," he went on, totally ignoring her outburst.

"Sorry!" She tried to duck out from under his hands, but his fingers only tightened on her shoulders, holding her in place.

"Yes, sorry," he repeated, his smile growing wider. "And a thank you, wouldn't hurt either," he suggested, lifting a hand to brush a wad of curls off her cheek. She tried to ignore the intimate gesture, but the reckless thud of her heart made Luke hard to ignore. His fingers were callused against her skin, but his touch was unbelievably gentle. She was shocked at the feminine instincts that throbbed to life at his simple touch. Bravely, Kati met his gaze. There was something in his eyes, something that caused her resentment to melt like wax under a flame.

"Oh, all right!" she finally grumbled, more annoyed at herself than at him. "I was wrong. I'm sorry. And thank you."

"Don't you ever get tired of handling everything yourself?" Luke asked, and Kati took a deep breath. His question caught her totally off guard.

She was strong—*now*. She had worked hard and long not to need or want anyone, ever, and she wasn't about to let one handsome blue-eyed son of a gun roar into her life unwelcome, and unwanted, and upset the settled order of things.

"No," she said firmly, shaking her head. "I don't need anyone."

"You don't?" Luke countered, sliding his hands to the nape of her neck. Slowly, he tilted her head back until she was forced to look at him. His blue eyes probed hers, wondering and asking, and Kati tried to turn away, knowing she couldn't—no *wouldn't* give him the answers he sought. Tension vibrated the air. "It's not a character flaw to need someone, Kati." His words were soft, his eyes kind, and Kati felt her heart flutter.

She would never be vulnerable again. *Never*, she reminded herself firmly. Not for this man, not for any man. She could not, and would not allow herself to depend on someone, to need someone, and then, be devastated when they up and disappeared.

Luke's gaze was searching her upturned face, probing, asking. Kati's eyes slid closed, trying to hide the emotions tearing through her. She had to remain calm, but it was hard. He was so close, her heart thundered in her breast. Never had she reacted so strongly to a member of the opposite sex.

Instinctively Kati knew that Lucas Kane was a different kind of man. He was the kind who needed to be in control, to call the shots, to have someone lean on him. Just from her response to him, Kati knew, Luke would be too easy for her to lean on. Now, it was more important than ever to get rid of him. The sooner the better.

"Kati, we have to settle this if we're going to work together," Luke said quietly, and her eyes flew open in panic.

"That's just the point, Luke," she said gravely. "We're not going to work together."

"Yes, we are," he countered smoothly, sliding his thumb across the delicate skin of her jaw. His touch caused the tight rein of control she had on her emotions to slip a notch, then another, as his feathery light touch delighted her skin.

"I don't want you here!" she said in exasperation, feeling more panicked by the moment, and trying to pretend that his touch wasn't affecting her.

"I know that," Luke said kindly. "But I'm staying." Luke was so close his breath whispered across her cheek. Frightened at the way the man made her feel, Kati realized she had to put some distance between them. Now. Before she did something foolish.

Lifting a hand to Luke's chest, Kati slowly began inching backward, but Luke matched her step for step.

"Luke," she finally managed to say as her back pressed against the swinging door. "I want you to know—" She stopped to draw a deep, shaky breath. "I want you to know, that this has got to stop. There will be no more repeats of last night," Kati announced firmly, hoping her voice was stronger than her willpower. "We're—we're business partners," she stammered, trying to ignore the shivers that bumped along her spine. "Nothing more."

"Kati Rose," Luke murmured, dipping his head close to hers. "I guarantee you that what's going on between us has *nothing* to do with business." Gently, he bent his head until his mouth was hovering just over hers. Their breaths mingled and her vulnerable heart jumped slightly in her chest. "What's between us is personal," he whispered. "*Very personal.*"

"There's nothing between us," she stammered weakly, trying to take another step back. But she couldn't. The blasted door was at her back. "What do you want?" she asked suddenly, instantly regretting her words at the look that softened his features.

"I want *you*, Kati," he said softly. There was something sad in his eyes. Something a bit forlorn that caused the walls of her heart to ache.

There couldn't be anything between them, her mind raged. He was the enemy! Too bad she forgot to tell her body that, she thought hazily.

"Luke—"

"Kati Rose!" Bessie yelled, pushing the swinging door into Kati's back and sending her tumbling awkwardly against Luke. Instinctively his arms went around her to steady her. For an instant she was pressed against the hard, muscular length of him and her pulse jumped wildly.

"You'd better hightail—" Bessie stopped abruptly when she caught sight of Kati in Luke's arms. A satisfied smile lifted her lips, and Kati stiffened.

"This isn't what it looks like," Kati stammered, trying to extract herself from Luke's embrace and stop the heat that was flooding her cheeks.

"Yes, it is," Luke countered wickedly, ignoring Kati's attempts to get free and keeping his arms firmly around her.

"Will you be quiet," Kati hissed, pushing him away and trying to gather her floundering composure. "What's the matter?" Kati asked Bessie, hoping it was something drastic so she could escape the confines of the kitchen. And Luke.

Bessie walked a circle around them, grinning and looking like there was a lot more than met the eye here, and she wasn't leaving until she figured out just what it was.

"Bessie?" Kati prompted impatiently.

"Vera and Mr. Billings are at it again," Bessie announced on a long, pain-filled sigh.

"Damnation!" Kati muttered, dragging a hand through her hair, and trying to inch further away from Luke without being obvious. "Now what? Don't tell me Mr. Billings brought Beauregard in with him again? If Tibbits gets wind of this, he'll close us down for good," she cried.

Luke's brows rose a fraction, and his eyes darkened in humor. He silently mouthed a word that Kati didn't understand. She was too fascinated with the soft fullness of his lips, too busy remembering what he had tasted like, to pay attention to what his lips were saying.

"What?" she demanded irritably.

"*Us?*" he said smoothly, and Kati swallowed a groan.

Damnation! She had used the term *us* without even thinking. Slip of the tongue, she assured herself, glaring at him and feeling as if she had just stepped into the spider's lair. An innocent mistake that meant nothing. Absolutely nothing. This was her diner, and hers alone, she reminded herself. Well, it would be once she got rid of *him*!

"If you two could stop your sparring for a minute," Bessie scolded, looking from one to the other, "I'll tell you what they're fussing about."

They both turned to stare at Bessie.

"That's better." She patted her gray head. "Poor old Beauregard's home getting his beauty sleep. Those two are arguing about who's gonna sit in that corner booth. I tried to tell them there are two corner booths, but for some reason they both want to sit in that one. You know how they are. Whatever one wants, so does the other. They're worse than babes. Those two aren't happy unless they're fussing about something," Bessie said pointedly, looking from Luke to Kati, as if she were speaking about *them*. "From the looks of things, I'd bet my pay they're ready to go the best two out of three, and I'm sure not gonna get in the middle of it."

"All right." Kati sighed, jamming a wad of hair back with her hand. "I'll handle it." She turned and strode toward the door, but Luke reached out his hand and stopped her.

"Why don't you let me handle it this time?" His gaze held hers and for a moment silence hung in the air as Kati's mind raced. Vera and Mr. Billings didn't take kindly to strangers. Particularly *interfering* strangers.

"All right, Luke," Kati said, trying not to smile. "You take care of it, I'll get started in here." For an instant she felt a twinge of guilt. It really wasn't fair to saddle Luke with her two most difficult customers. On the other hand, she reasoned, if the man wanted to be her partner, he might as well start learning right now.

Bessie waited until Luke was out of earshot before turning to her boss. "Kati Rose Ryan!" Bessie scolded, shaking her finger at her. "Now why'd you send him out there to deal with those two lunatics? You know how they feel about strangers." Bessie shook her gray head. "Honey, they're gonna chew that boy up and spit him out."

"I know," Kati said, grinning.

"Then why'd you—" Bessie stopped abruptly. "Why you little stinker!" Bessie chuckled softly. "Still trying to figure out a way to get rid of him, aren't you?"

"I don't need another partner." Kati sighed heavily, knowing that wasn't the only reason she had to get rid of Lucas Kane. "But I guess I'm just going to have to put up with him until he tires of the endless chores. I give him a week on the outside," she said confidently, crossing the room to peek through the little window of the swinging door.

"But Kati, surely you must know the man's intentions are honorable," Bessie protested. "Why, he even bought us a new stove."

"Just because the man bought me a new stove, doesn't mean I trust him," Kati said airily. "What's the old saying? Beware of men bearing gifts?"

Bessie chuckled softly. "Honey, that's not the way the saying goes."

Kati frowned. "It's close enough."

"Now what are you doing?" Bessie asked, trying to peek over Kati's shoulder.

"I want to watch the fireworks," she whispered, pressing her nose against the glass. "If I know Vera and Mr. Billings, Luke will be hightailing it back in here any second wondering why on earth he didn't just stay where he belonged."

"And you're gonna be enjoying every moment, aren't you?" Bessie asked, inching closer so she could watch the goings-on too. "Lordy, Kati Rose, that's terrible."

"I know," Kati said affectionately, tossing Bessie a smile.

"What on earth is that boy doing?" Bessie asked in bewilderment, trying to shoulder her way closer to the window so she could get a better view.

Kati's smile vanished. "I don't know."

Luke was wedged between Vera and Mr. Billings. If Kati's eyes weren't deceiving her, Vera was smiling up at Luke. Bowing formally at the waist, Luke took Vera's weathered hand in his, and gallantly kissed it. A faint tinge of pink rose to cover Vera's cheeks and her false eyelashes flapped like a flag in the breeze.

"What is he doing!" Kati hissed, her eyes widening in shock.

Vera took Luke's arm and allowed him to escort her to another booth in the corner. Luke bent and whispered something into Vera's ear that made the woman giggle girlishly. Fluttering her fake eyelashes, Vera preened up at Luke, a look of total adoration on her face.

Bessie whistled softly. "I don't know what he's doing, honey, but from where I'm standing it looks to me like he's charming the pants off of her. He sure must have a way with words. Haven't seen Vera flap her lashes that much since Fred the deliveryman told her she reminded him of Clara Bow."

"A way with words, indeed! Look out!" Kati cried, jumping back from the window and nearly knocking Bessie over. "He's coming. Look busy," she hissed frantically. "I don't want him to know we were watching him." Snatching a rag, Kati intently scrubbed the already gleaming counter. She pretended to be absorbed in her chore, but her attention and her ears were on the door.

"Well, I think we've taken care of the problem with Vera and Mr. Billings," Luke announced confidently. "I don't think we'll have any more problems with them."

Kati looked up at him, her face full of innocence. "Oh? What happened?"

Luke grinned and scratched the back of his neck. "They were fighting over who was going to sit in that booth. The suggestion that they share it didn't exactly draw applause. So I told Vera since she and Mr. Billings were both such good customers, it was only fair that they each have their own special booth. I assigned Vera that booth in the corner. Told her it was the best seat in the house, booth number one so to speak, and the only one befitting a lady of her great importance."

Bessie gave a gleeful snort, and Kati looked at him suspiciously. Aha! she thought. He's been here less than twenty-four hours and already he'd alienated Mr. Billings, one of her best customers. Surely that should convince the man he wasn't cut out for the diner business.

"I'm sure Vera loved that, Luke," she said reproachfully. "But I don't think Mr. Billings is going to be too pleased to know you gave the supposedly best booth in the house to Vera. *He's* one of our best customers, too." Rocking back on her heels, she smiled happily. This was going to be easier than she had first thought.

"Not at all, Kati. To tell you the truth, Mr. Billings loved the idea, since I assigned him a booth in the other corner and told him *he* had the best seat in the house."

"What!" The smile slid off her face. "You mean to tell me you convinced each of them they had the best booth in the house?"

"Sure did," Luke announced without a bit of remorse. "They both think they have booth number one and they're both happy as clams. Now let's hope that neither one finds out about the other," he whispered with a wink.

"I don't believe it!" Kati muttered, shaking her head.

"I've got to get back out there," Luke said brightly, trying not to smile at the look on her face. "Vera even offered me a place to stay until I got settled. She promised to tell me all about her days in the theater."

"She what?" Kati's face became a full-fledged scowl. This was not at all how things were supposed to turn out.

Grabbing an apron, Luke slid it on and headed toward the door. "Oh, by the way, Kati?"

"What?" she muttered glumly.

"The next time you want to keep an eye on me, but you don't want me to know—" he paused to flash her a knowing smile "—don't leave your nose prints on the glass." Lifting his apron, Luke wiped an imaginary smudge off the little window. Whistling softly, he pushed through the door.

"That—that—" Words failed her. At the moment, Kati couldn't think of a word appropriate enough, or nasty enough to call Lucas Kane.

"Kati Rose?" Bessie shoved her hands in her uniform and smiled, her gray eyes dancing wickedly. "I've got a feeling getting rid of Lucas Kane might be as easy as getting a long-legged chicken to lay hard-boiled eggs." Chuckling softly, Bessie sashayed out the door, leaving Kati alone with her frustrations.

Chapter Five

"Gonna hide out here in the kitchen the rest of your life?" Bessie inquired, backing into the room with a tray full of dirty dishes.

"I'm not hiding!" Kati declared indignantly, knowing all along that's exactly what she was doing.

But Luke was out there, in *her* diner! Still seething in frustration at the way Luke had outmaneuvered her with Vera and Mr. Billings this morning, Kati had dug her heels in, and tried to throw herself into her work. But it had been hard. How was she supposed to concentrate or do any work with the man constantly underfoot? Luke kept turning up everywhere. At her elbow when she fried bacon, behind her when she slid biscuits into the oven, and underfoot when she had ventured out front. If he smiled at her, or flashed that endearing grin of his at her one more time, she was going to scream! That smile could charm a baby out of its bottle!

Kati had tried to spend as much time as possible in the kitchen, venturing out front only when absolutely necessary. It was as if the battle lines were drawn and the door was the only thing that separated them. The kitchen was hers, the front serving area his. And that's the way she wanted it to stay. At least until she figured out a way to get him out of her diner and out of her life. Permanently!

If Lucas Kane thought his charm and disarming tactics were going to soften her, he was in for a rude surprise, she thought firmly. Surely she had grown immune to such tactics, hadn't she? Her brother Patrick was the best at charming and disarming, and no doubt he could probably teach Luke a thing or two.

"No need to get huffy, Kati. I was just asking." Bessie slid the tray of dishes onto one of the counters and mopped her brow with an exaggerated gesture. "It's sure been a hot one today." Bessie sighed heavily and something in her voice caused Kati to look up at her.

"Is something wrong, Bess?" Kati's brows gathered in concern as she looked at the woman carefully. "Are you feeling all right?"

"Nothing for you to worry about. I'm just feeling a little weak."

Kati's glance narrowed on the woman. Weak? Bessie? The woman was as healthy as a horse, and just about as stubborn. She'd never been sick a day in her life.

Bessie poured herself a glass of cool lemonade and downed it in one gulp, then mopped her brow again. "We'll be needing some more biscuits pretty soon," she announced, her voice strained and a bit pain-filled. "The dinner rush nearly cleaned us out." Bessie paused to fan her face, and Kati looked at her again.

"Bess? Are you sure you're all right?" Wiping her hands on her checkered apron, Kati leaned over and felt Bessie's forehead. The woman jumped back as if she'd been burned.

"No need worrying yourself about me, Kati Rose. I'm sure I'll be all right." Grabbing a load of clean dishes, Bessie shuffled toward the door, moving in slow motion. "Don't forget about those biscuits, now."

"I'll bring some out as soon as I'm finished here," Kati returned, her mind full of worry as she resumed peeling potatoes.

Maybe it had been too much to ask Bessie to initiate Luke into the routine of the diner, Kati thought with a twinge of guilt. She had asked Bessie to do it because she didn't trust herself to be around the man. The things he did to her nerves! The man's mere presence seemed to scramble her wits! There was something about him that caused her femininity to cry out.

If the truth be known, Kati wasn't quite sure who she was more annoyed at, herself or him! It wasn't just her temper that responded to the man. She caught herself listening for the sound of Luke's voice, or for his footsteps, or looking for his black head every time she ventured out front. Every time Luke did come into the kitchen, her heart would pound and her pulse would race.

Even when he wasn't in the room, the faint masculine aroma of him lingered in the air, driving her senses to distraction. She was letting her hormones overrule her reasoning, Kati decided, growing annoyed at herself all over again. She didn't have time for this nonsense.

"I simply don't!" she muttered, swiping at the potato again.

"They say people who talk to themselves have quite interesting conversations," Luke said from behind, causing Kati to scream. The potato and peeler went flying in the air.

Clutching her racing heart, Kati whirled around and glared at him. "I was not talking to myself," she snapped. "I was talking to—"

"Your potato?" he suggested helpfully, trying without success to squelch the grin that was threatening to break loose.

"Must you keep skulking around?" she demanded, more rattled than she cared to let on. Clamping her lips tightly shut, she bent over to scour the floor for her fallen items. Luke bent over at the same time and they bumped heads. Caught off balance, Kati started to tumble backward, but Luke grabbed her by the arms to steady her. Lifting her head, she pierced him with her gaze. If the man wasn't always underfoot maybe she wouldn't be so darn nervous!

"Kati?" He was talking to her like a petulant child, his voice soft and coaxing.

"What!" she snapped, unwilling to admit that the man's nearness was doing strange things to her inner system,

"I didn't skulk up on you," he said, grabbing her by the elbows and hauling her to her feet. "You were so busy talking to your—" he grinned "—potato, I guess you just didn't hear me." Luke bent over and retrieved her things from the floor. "Very nice," he commented rolling the mangled potato around in his hand and eyeing it mischievously. Kati snatched the hapless stub out of his hand.

"Did you want something?" she demanded crossly. He was just standing there staring at her, and she didn't have the faintest idea what to do with him. Well, she did, but Kati didn't think he'd take too kindly to her suggestion.

And more likely than not, Bessie'd wash her mouth out for even thinking such a thing.

"I believe we discussed what *I* wanted this morning," he said pointedly and Kati's heart clawed its way upward when she remembered what he wanted. *Her.* Heat ran the length of her, settling to warm her empty belly.

Kati's eyes slid closed. Damn the man! Why did he have the power to drag up these feelings in her? And why on earth wasn't she able to control them? Lord, he was only a man! And she'd never had any trouble handling *any* man before. They were all basically the same, weren't they? Irresponsible, allergic to work and given to flights of fancy and bouts of selfishness.

Slowly, her lids fluttered open and she chanced a peek at Luke. On the other hand, she'd never dealt with a man quite like Lucas Kane before. Just looking at the stubborn thrust of his handsome jaw, she had a feeling he wasn't going to be handled very easily.

"Damnation!" Kati muttered to herself, trying to shake away the disturbing thoughts.

"What was that?" Luke inquired mischievously, cupping his hand to his ear. "I didn't quite hear what you said."

"Nothing," she muttered glumly. "It was nothing."

Shoving his hands in the pockets of his well-worn jeans, Luke leaned back on his heels and looked at her. "You know, Kati, I think you've been working too hard. Talking to yourself, and now muttering under your breath. Maybe you need a vacation."

"What I need—" Kati stopped abruptly as his brows rose wickedly. Her face flamed at the amused glint in his eye. Clearly what *he thought she needed, and what she thought she needed* were two different things.

"Don't you have work to do?" she demanded irritably. Why on earth didn't the man back up a bit? He was standing so close. With her every breath his scent tempted and taunted her, burrowing deeper into her stunned senses.

"I'm doing it," he returned, lifting a finger to run it down her nose. "Peels," he commented, before she could open her mouth to protest. "There's a man out front to see you. Says his name is Barnwood. I believe he's your attorney." He looked at her knowingly, and Kati swallowed a groan.

Right after the fiasco with Vera and Mr. Billings, she had decided to call her attorney, Wilfred Barnwood, and have him check out the document Luke had presented her with. She seriously doubted the document was a fake, but still, with what was at stake, Kati had to be certain. What could it hurt? But she had never expected Wilfred to show up here. Didn't people believe in telephoning anymore?

"Tell him I'll be right out," she grumbled, grabbing a towel to wipe her hands in an effort to stop their trembling.

"Nice fellow," Luke said, reaching behind her to pick up a piece of potato. Popping it in his mouth, he chewed it gingerly. "Seems quite fond of you. We had a nice chat." Flashing her a wide smile, Luke turned and walked out the door, his boot heels clicking softly on the worn linoleum floor.

Kati's lips pursed in annoyance, wondering what on earth Wilfred would have to talk about with Luke. Unless it was *her, or her diner*.

"Men!" Kati muttered, yanking off her apron and hair net. Pausing to smooth back her wild tangle of auburn curls, she dug in her back pocket to make sure the paper

Luke had given to her last night was still there before pushing through the door.

It was just past the dinner rush and the diner was empty, except for Wilfred and a few straggling customers who were reading their evening papers and drinking coffee. The summer evening sun was setting, casting a hazy orange glow through the glass windows, bathing the diner in a muted warmth. Kati inhaled deeply. This was her favorite time of the day. Most of the day was gone, and she could relax, and finish up her work at her own pace. Her ragged nerves began to calm, until she spotted Luke.

"Wilfred, I believe you came here to see me," she said pointedly, nudging Luke aside.

"Evening, Kati Rose." Wilfred swept off his hat and bent to kiss her cheek. "How are you this fine Friday evening?"

She smiled at him and slid onto the next stool. He really was a dear man. With his handlebar mustache and his big, beefy features, Wilfred reminded her of a gentle walrus.

"I'm fine, Wilfred. And you?" she inquired politely, vividly aware that Luke was prowling around near them doing the evening set-ups.

"Just fine, dear. Just fine." He nodded toward Luke. "I had the pleasure of meeting your new partner. Seems like a fine young man." Wilfred smiled and Kati gritted her teeth.

"Did you check out that matter we discussed?" she asked quietly, not wanting Luke to overhear. Luke had rounded the counter and was busy washing out the coffee pots. There was no way he could not hear their conversation, and Kati grew instantly perturbed. Did the man have to be everywhere?

"Sure did. Talked to Luke's attorney, the man who drew up the papers. Let me see, now." Wilfred dug a small notebook out of his pocket and set his spectacles on his nose to examine his notes.

Bending closer, she whispered in Wilfred's ear. "Did you find out if the document is legal?"

Wilfred looked at her in surprise, his round eyes peering at her over the top of his glasses. "Why, Kati Rose, of course it is. It's perfectly legal. This here young man is your partner fair and square."

Her hopes dashed, Kati grasped at straws, not knowing how long she could resist Luke's charms.

"But Wilfred," she protested, "how on earth could Patrick sell his half of the diner without my permission?"

"Doesn't need your permission, honey, and he didn't sell it. Not outright. You and Patrick own the diner together, but as tenants-in-common. Either one of you can sell your half, or in this case, use it for collateral without the other's permission."

"You mean there's nothing I can do?" Kati cried, fearing all hope fade. "I'm stuck with him?" she hissed, nodding her head toward Luke.

Wilfred chuckled softly. "Well, honey, that's not quite how I'd put it, but to answer your question, yes. Unless of course you want to buy him out? I'd be happy to draw up the papers."

Kati shook her head. Buying Luke out was out of the question. She didn't have the capital to even consider such a thing. And borrowing was out of the question. After the fiasco with Everett yesterday, she'd be lucky if he ever talked to her again, let alone lend her money.

"Honey, it seems to me you'd be happy for a helping hand around here." At the stricken look on her face,

Wilfred reached out and patted her hand. "I'm sorry," he said sympathetically. "I didn't realize how much this news would upset you. But I'm sure everything will work out. Mr. Kane here seems like a fine young man. I know it hasn't been easy for you since your brother ran off, and I know you're used to doing things in your own way. You've had too much responsibility for too long, Kati Rose. It's not good for a pretty young thing like you to be so independent. Nothing wrong with needing some help now and then." Wilfred's face brightened and he flashed her a smile. "Might take some getting used to, but I'm sure you'll realize having someone else around to help you out just might be a blessing in disguise." Wilfred slid off his stool, plopped his straw hat atop his head and adjusted it comfortably. "If there's anything else I can do for you, you just give a holler, hear?" Wilfred pecked Kati on the cheek, flashed a smile at Luke, and strode out of the diner.

A blessing in disguise, Kati thought in disgust, glumly resting her chin in her hand. She watched Luke absently as he wiped down the counter. What was it about the man that made so-called normal, intelligent people fall under his spell?

All right, if she had to, she'd admit he was handsome. His features were rough-hewn and distinctively masculine. And, she admitted grudgingly, he was pleasant. She frowned. Disgustingly so. If the circumstances were different, she would no doubt find the man highly attractive, and quite appealing. Kati felt a wave of vexation settle over her. Who was she kidding? *In spite* of the circumstances, she found the man to be attractive, appealing, and a whole lot more. Perhaps, Kati mused, that was part of the problem. She felt threatened on all sides. Not only was her business at stake, and the independence she had worked so very hard to attain, but she had begun to fear that there might be something a bit more personal at stake as well. For some reason Lucas Kane seemed to make her more aware of her body, more aware of desires and yearnings too long denied. Kati knew she couldn't allow herself to respond to the man, no matter how charming. Too much was at stake.

"Kati?" Luke was bumping against her elbows with the wet rag. Obviously she was in his way.

"Sorry," she said absently, lifting her elbows so he could finish cleaning the counter.

"Something on your mind?" he inquired with a smile, watching as she stared off into space. Blinking, Kati looked at him and a slow, hot flush crept up her features. Why did she get the feeling Luke knew that *he* was on her mind?

"Nothing," she muttered, sliding off the stool and heading for the kitchen. She glanced around the diner and frowned. It was unusually quiet. Something was missing. "Luke, where's Bessie?"

"I sent her home."

Kati slowly turned around to face him, struggling to keep her face a calm mask. "You what?"

"I sent her home," Luke repeated slowly, drawing the words out carefully as if she were a bit dim-witted.

"How dare you!" she hissed, her words whistling through tightly clenched teeth. "How dare you presume to do such a thing without even consulting me? This is my diner, and I don't want you issuing orders over my head or without checking with me first."

"Our diner," he corrected with a long sigh, trying not to smile at her furious face.

"Who the hell do you think you are?" Kati faced him, drawing herself up to her full five feet *nothing* height, stretching her spine and vainly wishing she could pull herself up to five feet *something*. Her rage grew stronger at the hint of a smile that played along his mouth. "Why don't you just go back where you came from?"

One dark brow lifted in amusement. "Now why do I get the feeling you just told me where to go?" he asked, his grin widening. "And I don't think it's the same place I came from."

Kati opened her mouth, fully intending to tell him in very unladylike terms just exactly where he could go. But she didn't get the chance.

"Let's discuss this in the kitchen," Luke ordered, his tone of voice causing the words to evaporate from her lips. Luke clamped his fingers down on her arm and dragged her through the swinging door and into the kitchen, deliberately ignoring her howls of protest.

"Take your hands off of me!" Kati yelled, trying to shake loose of him. He held on tight, releasing her only after he had backed her up against the gleaming silver counter. Kati couldn't move, there was no place to go, unless she wanted to climb over the counter. Or over him, which she seriously considered. For a moment. Until she saw the look on his face. Her temper immediately ebbed away, replaced by a bout of good old-fashioned fear. He was looming over her from his imperial height and she didn't particularly care for the look on his face. It was a combination of anger and amusement, and she didn't know which one was worse.

"Kati Rose," he finally said, his voice low and deadly calm. He leaned down until he was eyeball-to-eyeball with her, and Kati blinked self-consciously. "I am your partner," he said slowly, making no move to back away and give her some breathing room. "And whether you like it or not, I am here to stay." He lifted a hand and captured her chin, forcing her to look at him. "If you would have let me explain before you went off on a tangent, you would have learned that I sent Bessie home because she wasn't feeling well."

Kati's eyes rounded in stunned surprise. "What? Well for goodness' sakes!" Kati frowned. "Why didn't Bessie tell *me* she wasn't feeling well?" she asked in confusion.

"Because she told *me*," he countered calmly. His thumb traced a lazy pattern on her chin, distracting her a bit.

"Why on earth would she tell *you*?" she demanded, clearly not understanding and feeling more threatened by the moment. The man had waltzed into her life, and now suddenly seemed to be taking over!

Luke sighed and straightened his frame. "You know very well Bessie wouldn't tell you that she didn't feel well. She knows how much you depend on her. I practically had to throw her out of here," he countered calmly, all traces of his temper gone.

Guilt engulfed her and Kati glumly dropped her chin to stare at the tiled floor. Bessie was sick and she didn't even tell *her*! Perhaps, Kati mused darkly, if she hadn't been caught up in her own problems with Luke this morning she would have realized Bessie wasn't well. From the moment the man had entered her life, he had seemed to be trying to gain control, trying to take over! He had conned Tibbits, bought her a new stove, handled Vera and Mr. Billings, and now he had gained Bessie's confidence. He had presumed to issue orders over her head, without even bothering to consult her! She could feel her business slipping quickly through her hands and into his, and she didn't like it, not one bit!

"Kati?" He tipped her chin upward so she was forced to meet his eyes again. "All you've done since I've arrived is tell me what you *don't* want. Why don't you tell me what you do want?"

"What I want," she said shakily, trying to ignore what his touch was doing to her, "is for you to leave."

"Sorry." He smiled, letting his thumb drift to outline her bottom lip. "I have my reasons for staying."

"What reasons?" she stammered, trying hard to hang on to her anger.

"Reasons that are none of your business," he countered, holding her gaze, and slowing the pattern of his thumb to a sensual tease.

"Everything about this diner is my business," she stammered, as shock waves of longing licked up her skin, raising the fine hair on her neck and her arms.

"And mine," he said evenly, and Kati struggled to find her fluttering anger. Must the man be so all-fired stubborn! "Kati." Luke sighed heavily. "With Bessie out sick, we've got no choice but to work together and try to get along. I promised Bessie I'd take over her chores for her. It's the only way I could get her to go home."

"You?" she cried incredulously, not willing to admit that the idea of working alone with him day after day just might be too much for her to handle. With Bessie there, at least she had a buffer; with her gone, there would be nothing but her and him. The thought brought on a frisson of alarm, and her determination to get rid of him grew by leaps and bounds.

"You think you're going to be able to take over for her? You don't know anything about the diner business and you think you can just walk right in and take her place?" Maybe she could insult him into leaving. But the look on his face dashed that hope, quickly.

"Something funny about that?" One dark brow rose in challenge. "Whether you like it or not, with Bessie gone, you have no choice but to depend on me. Someone has to take over Bessie's work. You certainly can't do everything yourself, even though you'd like to think you can." He smiled lazily, and her temper flared again. "Like it or not," Luke said, working a lazy pattern on her lips with his fingers. "You need me."

"Need you!" she hissed. Kati inhaled deeply, and her eyes blazed. "Lucas Kane," she roared. "It will be a cold day in hell when I—" His mouth caught the rest of her tirade as he jerked her to him, nearly knocking the wind from her. His lips possessed hers, forcing her to respond. Kati raised her hands to his chest to push him away, but instead, she found her arms crawling around his neck, her fingers burying themselves in the thick mat of dark silky hair. Her traitorous lips responded to his, giving back and taking everything he had to offer. His lips tightened, working over hers with a gentleness that astounded her.

Luke's hands roamed freely from the small circle of her waist, bringing her body close to his until she felt the warmth and hardness of him pressed against her soft curves. His mouth drugged her, taking and draining all her anger. She felt herself turn pliant in his arms, sagging against him as his lips seared hers, branding and possessing her. Bone-melting hunger, swift and fierce, settled over her, seeping through her pores, and shimmying across every nerve ending.

He was the enemy, her mind raged. But, Kati realized a bit belatedly, she had forgotten to tell her heart.

"Luke, honey," a feminine voice called as the kitchen door swung open. Luke lifted his head, pulling his lips from Kati's just as MayBelle Watson stuck her head through. "Here you are," MayBelle purred. "I thought you were going to get me something cool to drink. You *know* how hot I get, sugar."

"I'll be right out, MayBelle," Luke commented, not taking his eyes off Kati's. His eyes were sending her a message, but she was too dazed to read it clearly. Panting softly, Kati licked her swollen lips in sudden nervousness, savoring the taste of Luke that still clung to her lips. She tried to look away, tried to break the contact that still connected her to him, but found she couldn't. His eyes held hers just as captive as his lips had a moment ago. Where was her resolve when she needed it, she wondered glumly?

"I'll be waiting, sugar. Don't keep me waiting," MayBelle purred, before letting the door swing shut behind her.

"MayBelle's waiting for you," Kati reminded him stiffly, trying not to let on that she was intensely curious about what was going on between Luke and MayBelle. It wasn't any of her business, she reminded herself, to no avail.

"Let her wait," Luke returned calmly, and her gaze turned into a glare.

"But she wants something cool to drink!" All she wanted was to get him out of her kitchen and out of her vision so she could try to think, try to breathe, and try to figure out just what to do with him.

"What MayBelle wants," Luke said, holding her gaze and trying not to grin, "*is me*."

Stunned, Kati stared at him wide-eyed for a moment. "Why you arrogant, insufferable man!" Her emerald eyes blazed in fury as she gave him a good thump on the chest. "You think *I need you* in my diner, and MayBelle wants you in her bed! Is there no end to your conceit?"

Luke chuckled softly. "I'm not interested in what MayBelle wants," Luke returned, not in the least bit daunted by her fury. "But I am interested in *you*. If you'll just stop fighting me, you'll see we can be good together." His insufferable tone grated at her raw nerves. She had a feeling he wasn't just talking about their relationship at the diner, either. "You need me," he added firmly, and Kati's temper erupted.

Lucas Kane didn't know it, but he had just issued an open declaration of war! She didn't want or need him, and she was going to do everything in her power to prove it to him!

"We'll just see about that," she snapped smugly, ducking around him and heading toward the door. "We'll just see!"

Chapter Six

Kati Rose! Where's that refill of coffee you promised me?" Mr. Billings yelled. "And what'd you put in this here sandwich? I asked for roast beef, and this looks like tuna!" Mr. Billings wrinkled his nose in disdain as he inspected the sandwich Kati had slapped on the table in front of him just moments before. "Smells like tuna, too," he grumbled, taking a big sniff.

Sighing in exasperation, Kati snatched the coffee pot from behind the counter, trying to juggle the pot and several empty bowls as she hurried over to his table and poured him a refill.

"This coffee's cold," Mr. Billings complained after taking a quick sip. "And this here's a tuna sandwich. I ordered beef."

"Eat it. It's good for you," Kati scolded, moving on to the next table to clear it. She slammed the coffee pot on the dirty table and looked longingly at the booth. Oh, what blessed bliss if she could just sit down for a moment. She'd been handling the kitchen, the front *and* the customers for two long days, ever since Luke had sent Bessie home. If the relationship between her and Luke had been a battle before, now it was a full-scale war. She was determined to prove that she didn't need him. And he was just as determined to prove she did. At this moment, she had to admit the score was ten to nothing, in favor of Luke. He had been dogging her steps, cleaning up after her mistakes, and handling the things she just didn't have time for. Her mind always seemed to be three steps ahead of her feet.

Wiping her brow with the back of her hand, she started clearing the table. Out of the corner of her eye, she saw Luke approach Mr. Billings' table, take his sandwich and head toward the kitchen. She quickly finished clearing the table, grateful at least that the day was half over.

Carrying the tray of dirty dishes into the kitchen, Kati glanced at Mr. Billings' table. Luke had given him a new sandwich, roast beef this time, and it looked like he had made fresh coffee, too.

Kati dumped the dishes on the counter, as a sudden inexplicable wave of gratitude washed over her. Under any other circumstances she would have been graciously appreciative of all of Luke's help, and normally would have gone out of her way to thank the man. But these weren't other circumstances, she reminded herself.

The phone rang, and with a weary sigh, she crossed the kitchen to snatch the receiver.

"Hello?"

"Kati, this is O'Brien's Dairy. We had a fire out here last night. Not too bad, but it will be a few days before we can make any deliveries."

Her eyes slid shut and Kati swore softly under her breath. She had always dealt with the local small businessmen. A small business owner herself, she appreciated the loyalty of her customers. Occasionally there were problems with deliveries and such, but it had never been anything she couldn't work around. It was worth a little inconvenience in order to patronize the small businesses in the area. Normally, she'd leave Bessie in charge of the diner and drive over to pick up the needed items herself. But Bessie wasn't here, and she had no idea how she was going to get the supplies she needed.

"Kati? Are you still there?"

She pressed her hand to her eyes. "I'm still here. I'm sorry about the fire, Ralph," she said, cursing Mother Nature and every other entity she could think of. "Hope everyone's fine?"

"They are. No one got hurt. But thanks for asking. I'm sorry about this, Kati, but I'm really short-handed and the place is a mess. Your stuff's all ready, I just don't have anyone to come deliver it. We'll be open until four today if you want to come get the stuff yourself."

Kati glanced quickly at the large wall clock. It was after two already. She still had pork to roast for the dinner rush. If she hurried, she might just make it to get the supplies she needed for tomorrow's breakfast rush. But what about the diner? She couldn't just up and waltz out of here.

"Thanks, Ralph. I'll be there," she said firmly, hanging up the receiver and having no idea how she'd get there. Unless she asked Luke to... No, she quickly banished the thought.

"Kati Rose!" Mr. Billings' voice wafted through the door.

"Damnation!" she muttered, pushing through the door. Now what?

"Where's my egg custard?" Mr. Billings called. "Today's Thursday, Kati Rose, and you know I always have egg custard on Thursday." Kati slapped a hand to her forehead. She had a brand new oven but it certainly didn't work unless she put something into it.

"No egg custard today, Mr. Billings." She flashed him and Vera a sheepish smile. They were looking at her very strangely. They had been looking at her like that all week long. "Sorry. How about a nice bowl of ice cream?" she asked, looking from one face to the other.

"Now, Kati Rose, you know Mr. Billings doesn't like ice cream," Vera scolded.

"When's Bessie coming back?" Mr. Billings asked, searching the room for Luke.

"I don't know," Kati admitted with a shrug of her shoulders. She'd been wondering the same thing herself. Kati only hoped Bessie would return soon. Very soon.

"Well, you let me know when she does," Mr. Billings grumbled, getting to his feet. "Maybe when she gets back things will return to normal. And then *we'll* be back." Kati stood stock still, staring as Mr. Billings and Vera headed for the door. But Luke came through the kitchen door, took one look at Kati's wretched face and Mr. Billings' scowl, and headed toward the duo. Luke caught up with them just as they reached the door. Kati couldn't hear what they were saying, but Mr. Billings and Vera were both smiling as they turned around and slid back into the booth.

Flashing her a wink, Luke ducked behind the counter and returned with two dishes of ice cream, which Vera and Mr. Billings accepted with a happy smile.

Sighing, Kati turned and headed back into the kitchen, feeling more dejected by the minute. Even her most loyal customers seemed to have crossed over to the enemy! she thought with a bit of resentment. Who could blame them? she wondered miserably.

Kati opened the refrigerator door and stopped abruptly. Where was the pork she'd been marinating? Oh Lord, how could she lose twenty-two pounds of pork? Her gaze darted around the kitchen.

Curiously following her nose, she opened the oven door, and found the missing pork. Annoyance tightened her lips. Luke again. He must have put the meat in for her while she was clearing the tables. She looked at the gleaming counters. Where were the dirty dishes she'd left? The kitchen was clean, except for a lone coffee pot that had to be hand-washed. The gentle hum of the dishwasher told her Luke had loaded the dishwasher for her, too. Luke. He seemed to be everywhere.

Sighing, Kati leaned her elbows on the counter and rested her head in her hands. The blasted man was wearing her resistance down. It was hard to maintain her resentment when the man was being so darn helpful. Luke had sailed into her well-ordered boring life and within days had firmly entrenched himself into all of her affairs, turning everything upside down.

She couldn't keep this up much longer, Kati realized. She was tired of fighting Luke at every turn. It took far too much of her energy, energy better spent elsewhere. But her pride was at stake. It had been childish of her to behave so badly, she realized a bit belatedly. She let her vicious temper get the best of her. Common sense flew out the window the moment her temper began to rise. After the way she'd treated Luke, she was surprised he had even bothered to help her.

Kati smiled; she'd been so wrong about this man. Luke was a worthy opponent, and showed no more sign of giving in than she did. But one of them was going to have to give in, and soon. She had a sneaking suspicion it was not going to be Lucas Kane. She'd finally met someone as stubborn as she.

Luke had met her head-on and never backed down. The man took everything she dished out and showed no more inclination of bolting than she did. Obviously Lucas Kane wasn't afraid of a little hard work. It was refreshing, and Kati couldn't help but admire the man.

Perhaps it was time to call for a truce, Kati decided, jumping up to pace the kitchen. Yes, a truce might just be the thing. Hadn't her father always told her if you couldn't beat 'em, join 'em? They would both save face, and surely it would only improve things around here. Luke was a formidable opponent, and a worthy one, but Kati had a feeling it would be better to have him on her side, than against her. But how on earth could she manage a truce, without surrendering?

"Kati?"

The soft sound of Luke's voice brought her feet to an abrupt stop. He was standing right behind her; she could feel the warmth of his body heat, smell the faintly musky aroma of him.

"Kati?" He touched her shoulders hesitantly. "Are you all right?" His voice was so full of concern, she smiled. Or tried to.

"I'm fine," she managed to get out. She turned to face him. "I've been thinking..." Her voice trailed off at the look on his face. She would be perfectly content to stand here and stare at him for the rest of the day.

"What were you thinking about?" he asked. He had a towel thrown over his shoulder and an apron tied around his middle. And he looked right at home.

Deliberately, she turned her gaze to the ceiling, hoping to find some courage or some answers. She found neither. "I have a proposition for you," she stammered, as one dark brow rose in amusement.

"A proposition?" Luke repeated. His voice lilted with humor and Kati scowled.

"Not *that* kind of proposition!" she scolded, feeling her face flame.

"Pity," he said matter-of-factly and the tone of his voice made her heart skip an unsteady beat. Luke's eyes danced wickedly as they searched her face. How on earth was she going to get this out if he didn't stop teasing her? Didn't he realize how hard this was for her?

Kati took a deep breath, squared her shoulders and lifted her chin. "I think it's time to call a truce," she said quietly. If the man laughed at her, or so much as smiled, she was going to smack him!

"A truce?" he repeated, rolling the word around on his tongue as if trying it out for size. "Does this mean that you're ready to give up? Throw in the white towel and cry surrender?" he inquired happily and Kati stiffened.

"Well, you don't have to gloat about it," she snapped. The man had a way of igniting her temper with just a few simple words.

"Well, are you?" he inquired, making no attempt to hold the smile from his lips.

"Am I what?" she returned, stalling for time. Luke leaned down and pressed his face close to hers. Her heart immediately began to flutter and her thoughts fragmented. He was so close she could see the way his eyes darkened, see the smile lines along his mouth. His mouth, she thought hazily, was so full, so soft. If she leaned forward just a bit, she'd be able to touch her mouth to his.

"Are you ready to admit you were wrong about me?" he asked softly, making no attempt to move back. His eyes searched hers, and Kati knew she could do nothing but tell the truth with him so close, with his eyes probing hers.

"Yes," she whispered. He was standing too close to her and she could barely force her lungs to work. "I was wrong."

"And," he continued, his voice soft and warm, his breath dancing off her skin. "Are you willing to admit you need me?"

Kati stared into Luke's eyes, dizzy from all the emotions racing through her. She needed him, she realized suddenly, and not just in the diner.

"Yes," she whispered, feeling off balance. Kati turned her back to him, wanting nothing more than to break the spell that seemed to be drawing her closer and closer to him. She didn't want him to see her need, her personal need anyway. Not until she tried to sort it out for herself.

He touched her shoulder. "Kati?" He waited for her to turn around and face him again. Taking a shaky breath, she turned and met his gaze, realizing she was just as susceptible to his charm as every other female. "I know how hard that was for you. Thank you." His voice was sincere now, with no trace of humor, and she smiled, grateful at least that he hadn't made a fool of her. Her admiration for him grew. And then grew some more.

"A truce, then." He held out his hand and Kati stared at it. Finally, she laid her hand in his and he tugged her gently, pulling her close. With a relieved sigh she went into his arms and laid her head on his shoulder. Having someone to lean on, to depend on, did have its benefits.

Her instincts about the man had been right. Lucas Kane wasn't a man that could be handled, not by her, not by anyone. Perhaps that's what made him so appealing.

The more
you love romance . . .
the more
you'll love this offer

FREE!

Mail this heart today! (See inside)

Join us on a Silhouette® Honeymoon
and we'll give you
4 free books
A free manicure set
And a free mystery gift

IT'S A
SILHOUETTE HONEYMOON —
A SWEETHEART
OF A FREE OFFER!

HERE'S WHAT YOU GET:

1. Four New Silhouette Romance® Novels — FREE!

Take a Silhouette Honeymoon with your four exciting romances — yours FREE from Silhouette Books. Each of these hot-off-the-press novels brings you the passion and tenderness of today's greatest love stories . . . your free passports to bright new worlds of love and foreign adventure.

2. A compact manicure set — FREE!

You'll love your beautiful manicure set — an elegant and useful accessory to carry in your handbag. Its rich burgundy case is a perfect expression of your style and good taste — and it's yours free with this offer!

3. An Exciting Mystery Bonus — FREE!

You'll be thrilled with this surprise gift. It will be the source of many compliments, as well as a useful and attractive addition to your home.

4. Free Home Delivery!

Join the Silhouette Romance subscriber service and enjoy the convenience of previewing 6 new books every month delivered right to your home. Each book is yours for only $1.95. And there is no extra charge for postage and handling. Great savings plus total convenience add up to a sweetheart of a deal for you!

5. Free Newsletter!

You'll get our monthly newsletter, packed with news on your favorite writers, upcoming books, even recipes from your favorite authors.

6. More Surprise Gifts!

Because our home subscribers are our most valued readers, we'll be sending you additional free gifts from time to time — as a token of our appreciation.

START YOUR SILHOUETTE HONEYMOON TODAY — JUST COMPLETE, DETACH AND MAIL YOUR FREE-OFFER CARD

Get your fabulous gifts
ABSOLUTELY FREE!

MAIL THIS CARD TODAY.

PLACE
HEART STICKER
HERE

GIVE YOUR HEART
TO SILHOUETTE

Yes! Please send me my four Silhouette Romance novels FREE, along with my free manicure set and free mystery gift as explained on the opposite page.

NAME _____
　　　　　(PLEASE PRINT)

ADDRESS _____ APT. _____

CITY _____ STATE _____

ZIP CODE _____

215 CIL HAXJ

Prices subject to change. Offer limited to one per household and not valid to present subscribers.

SILHOUETTE BOOKS "NO-RISK" GUARANTEE

— There's no obligation to buy — and the free books and gifts remain yours to keep.

— You receive books before they appear in stores.

— You may end your subscription any time — just write and let us know.

START YOUR
SILHOUETTE HONEYMOON TODAY.
JUST COMPLETE, DETACH AND MAIL YOUR
FREE-OFFER CARD.

If offer card below is missing, write to:
Silhouette Books, 901 Fuhrmann Blvd., P.O. Box 9013, Buffalo, N.Y. 14240-9013

He was different from her brother Patrick, and any of her brother's other friends. Lucas Kane was a different kind of man in every sense of the word. He had stood toe to toe with her and never backed down.

"Luke?" The word came out a breathy whisper as she raised her head to look at him. "I'm sorry." Remorse and shame caused a lump to form in her throat. She wasn't a mean or cruel person. Just a scared one. More scared of this man than any other. Scared of him and the feelings she felt for him. Perhaps that's why she had wanted to get rid of him, before it was too late. She realized now, it was already too late.

"It's all right," Luke murmured. "It's not a criminal offense to need someone, Kati. We all do at one time or another." He was trying to make this easy for her. But if she wanted them to have a fresh start, a real truce, then she'd have to clear the air, and her conscience.

"I'm not sorry about needing you," she explained. "I'm sorry about the way I've treated you." Nodding, Luke tightened his arms around her and urged her head back down on his shoulder. His hand stroked the back of her head, his words as soothing as his touch. Taking a shuddering breath, Kati reveled in the scent of him. Lord, he smelled so good. Felt so good. His heady scent seemed to daze her senses, and she buried her face closer, wanting only to stay here, enveloped in the protectiveness of his arms.

He smiled, and reaching in his back pocket for a handkerchief, lifted her face and wiped at the tears she hadn't known were there.

"Thank you," she murmured, dragging up a shaky smile and wishing she could just stay here in his arms forever. The thought shocked her and she blinked up at him, surprised at the intensity of her own feelings.

"I'd better go back out front, Kati. We've still got work to do."

"Do you think you could go to the dairy and pick up a delivery?" she asked, holding her breath and waiting to see how he would react. She'd never actually asked him outright to do anything.

"I'll take my truck and go get the supplies. Do you think you can handle things until I get back?"

Sniffling, Kati nodded, unwilling to let go of his shirt just yet. Unwilling to let *him* go just yet. Just having him there, knowing he was going to help her brought on a tidal wave of relief.

"You don't know how to get there," she remembered with a frown.

"So you'll give me directions. I'd like to leave soon. Are you sure you'll be all right until I get back?" he asked, lifting a finger to wipe another fallen tear.

Kati smiled and nodded her head. She was going to be fine. Now.

"Luke?" she asked hesitantly. "Do you think you can stop at the bank and make a deposit for me?"

"Sure thing." Luke smiled. "You just make a list of all the things you want me—"

"Oh Luke, honey?" MayBelle's voice floated in through the door and Luke groaned softly.

"Damn!" He jammed a hand through his hair.

"What's wrong?" Kati asked hurriedly, unaccustomed to seeing Luke flustered.

"It's MayBelle." His voice dropped to a whisper. "Kati, now don't get mad. I didn't want to hurt her feelings so I told her—" He stopped and grinned. The smile lit up his blue eyes and Kati found herself smiling in return.

"What? What did you tell her?" Kati asked, her curiosity aroused.

His grin widened. "I told her that...well...now don't get mad, but I told her that there was more to our relationship than just business."

"You what?" Kati cried and Luke clamped a hand over her mouth and started to laugh.

"Shhh," he whispered, trying to talk around his laughter as he bent to speak in her ear. "Don't get mad," he whispered, his voice warm and soft against her ear, causing her toes to curl inside her shoes. "I didn't know what else to do. Will you help me out here?"

His hand was still clamped over her mouth and her eyes widened. Luke had told her the truth. Apparently he really wasn't interested in MayBelle. Her spirits soared.

If Luke was going to be such a good sport about helping her out, especially—no, particularly—after the way she had treated him, the least she could do was help him out of a jam with MayBelle. MayBelle was a bit blowsy and overblown, man-crazy no doubt, but she was sweet and kind, and wouldn't hurt a fly. Kati felt a wave of sympathy for the poor woman, but felt even more sympathy for Luke. MayBelle could be *very* persistent when she set her mind to something, Kati remembered, thinking about the way the woman had pursued her brother Patrick.

"Will you?" Luke prompted, making no attempt to remove his hand from her mouth. Kati nodded and Luke released her. Over her shoulder she saw MayBelle's red hair a moment before the door swung open.

"Kiss me quick!" Kati ordered, grabbing the front of Luke's shirt again and pulling him down close. "She's coming!"

Luke's eyes widened in delighted surprise a moment before his lips found hers. She didn't even hear the door open as his full mouth took possession of hers. She slid her hands from his chest, up the powerful muscles of his arms, her fingertips tingling from the strength of his firm skin.

Luke's mouth opened, his tongue gently tracing the outline of her lips and Kati trembled as a rush of desire and a million other sensations washed over her, leaving her breathless. His sweet tongue gently probed, tasting the soft warm surface of her mouth and she arched closer to him, wanting nothing more than to feel him everywhere. His hands slid a maddening path from her waist to her shoulders. Her breasts were crushed against his powerful chest, the rapid thud of his heart racing, and matching the rate of her own.

With a muffled groan, Luke lifted his head. "Oh, Kati Rose," he murmured, and she blushed, the heat rising from her neck to flood her cheeks. His eyes slid over her, caressing her as gently as his hands had, just moments before.

"I'd better get to the bank and the dairy," he said gruffly. He turned, but Kati reached out and touched his arm, her hand sizzling from the contact.

"Luke?"

He turned and his eyes snared hers, settling on the soft satin of her mouth. Her breath seemed to wedge in her throat. "Thank you," she whispered.

"You're welcome." Smiling, Luke turned and headed out the door. Kati could hear MayBelle's voice as he entered the front serving area and she smiled, remembering what Luke had said.

She *did* need him, and MayBelle *did* want him in her bed. Kati laughed softly. Lucas Kane had been right all along.

"Mmm, something smells good." Luke pushed through the kitchen door, a tray of plates in his hand and a wide, disarming smile on his face.

Kati laughed softly. "It's my bread pudding."

"No, it's not," Luke said, coming up behind her and dipping his head close to hers. "Vanilla always did drive me wild." A shiver raced through her as Luke's warm breath skittered across her neck. She tried not to notice how close he was, or how sensitized her body was to his nearness.

"Kati, what's wrong?" Luke asked suddenly, his voice tinged with worry.

She let out her breath slowly, knowing he was standing right behind her, knowing if she turned, he'd be there, waiting. In the past week, ever since the day she had asked Luke for his help, things had changed between them. There was a warmth, an electricity that seemed to draw them together, and Kati was powerless to stop it.

"It's nothing," she lied, aware that her voice was thin and slightly breathless. "Why?"

"Because you're putting dirty dishes in the oven." Luke leaned forward, plucked the dishes free, then set them down on the counter. Kati stared vacantly at the mess, convinced she was losing her mind as well as her heart.

"Following this reasoning," Luke commented, crossing the room, "I can't wait to see what's in the dishwasher." One dark black brow rose, and Luke gave her a playful grin as he extracted the pan of bread pudding from the bottom of the dishwasher. "I knew there was a certain logic to this. It just took me a minute to figure it out." There was no reproach in his voice, only mild amusement, and a heated warmth laced Kati's cheeks.

Valiantly, she struggled to think of a good reason to give Luke for her erratic behavior. She couldn't very well tell him the truth! What could she say? His presence was so distracting she didn't know what she was doing anymore? That the only thing on her mind was him? No, she couldn't very well admit that to the man, even if it was the truth.

In the past week, she had tried to keep her mind on her own chores, but it was hard. No, her mind corrected, it was downright impossible. Luke was always around and always in her thoughts. Her attention span was about as long as a minute and there was a restlessness in her that she didn't understand. With just a look, just a touch, the man had the ability to scramble her wits!

When she closed her eyes, she saw his face, his beautiful smile. His scent lingered to tease her. Her body hungered for his touch. She would lie in bed, wide awake, watching the clock creep slowly along, knowing each hour would bring her closer to seeing him again, and feeling the familiar sense of dread and anticipation. Dread because she knew that with each passing day her feelings for him were growing, and had nothing to do with business. And anticipation because just seeing him, just his presence seemed to bring a lightness to her step, a happiness to her heart.

"Kati? What is it?" His deep voice dropped an octave and she could sense his concern.

She looked up at him and flashed him a sheepish smile. "I guess I've been a bit...preoccupied," she finished lamely, feeling like a fool.

"Is that all? Are you sure it's not something else?" His brows furrowed in concern as his eyes scanned her features. She was still too pale for his tastes, and she still had those damn shadows under her eyes. "Kati, if there's a problem with the diner, if you're worried about something, tell me. You know you can always count on me."

Luke had been pulling his weight and doing more than his fair share, and she'd spent the better part of her time walking around in circles, not knowing if she was coming or going, but worse, not even caring!

He cradled her face in his hands. "You know I'm always here to help. Whatever it is, you can tell me." His thumbs caressed her chin, encouraging her to look at him and the familiar feelings of longing engulfed her, weakening her knees.

"I know," she said gravely, avoiding his eyes. That was the problem. Luke was always there, and always in her thoughts. Taking a deep breath, she tried to get her mind back on track. She couldn't remember when she'd been so out of sorts. Perhaps it was because he was so close.

"Could you back up a bit?" she asked suddenly, and Luke chuckled, but made no move to back up.

"Why?" he asked gently. "Are you afraid of me, Kati Rose Ryan?" He had used her full name and it sounded so wonderful rolling off his lips.

"A little bit," she admitted. Afraid wasn't quite the right word, but it would have to do for now.

"Why?"

Kati swallowed around the sudden dryness in her throat. Dropping her chin, Kati stared glumly at her tennis shoes.

"Kati?" he prompted, brushing his thumbs against her chin and encouraging her to look at him. Her breath fled as her eyes found his.

"Because you—I—"

"Because you know that there's a lot more between us than just the diner?" he asked softly, letting his fingers slide up to caress her cheeks.

Nodding, Kati couldn't pull her gaze from his. She could feel his eyes touching, caressing every intimate detail of her face. Her skin burned, her lips ached and tingled, wanting, waiting for the touch of his.

"Does that scare you, Kati?" He needed to know if she was still afraid of him. Trust. He needed hers more than he'd ever needed anything. Or anyone. But he didn't want her fear.

"Yes." She gave a shaky laugh, feeling an enormous amount of relief that it was finally out in the open.

"Don't be scared, Kati," Luke said softly. "I won't hurt you, Kati. Not ever." Smiling, Luke slid his arms around her. The air in the kitchen seemed suddenly still, thick. Kati licked her lips in sudden nervousness and Luke's eyes followed the movement of her tongue. Kati tried to take a deep breath, to loosen the increasing pressure around her heart, but she found she couldn't; the air short-circuited before it reached her throat.

Taking a long, shuddering breath, Luke's lips found hers, and Kati felt her heart thud recklessly in her breast. His lips were slow, gentling, and she felt her limbs and every other part of her relax as languid splendor sapped at her strength. She slid her arms around his neck, feeling his muscles flex as his arms caressed her, held her. She lost herself in his touch, his scent, his caress.

Luke lifted his head too soon, and her eyes fluttered slowly open, darkened by passion, darkened by need. Luke took a step back, admonishing himself. He knew better. He had to go slow. Slower. And if he didn't get out of here, out of this kitchen, he wouldn't be able to think, let alone reason.

"I won't hurt you," Luke promised, dropping his mouth to hers to give her a quick kiss before turning and heading for the door.

Kati stared after him, absently touching her swollen lips. She had lost the battle, and the war, and was now firmly entrenched in enemy territory. So why, she wondered with a bright smile, was she so happy?

Chapter Seven

Lemon-splashed sunlight filtered through Kati's bedroom. She rolled over and opened her eyes, groaning softly. It wasn't the sun that had woken her up, but something else. What? Yawning sleepily, she sat up and brushed her hair out of her eyes. Her arm froze as she heard the sound again. Her eyes darted to her bedroom window. If she didn't know better, she'd swear someone was throwing stones at her window! Sitting perfectly still, she waited. There it was again! Throwing off the covers, Kati didn't bother with a robe as she marched across the room fully determined to put an end to whatever prankster was ruining her sleep. Morning was not her best time, particularly *Sunday* morning, which was the one day of the week when she could sleep late. Unless some rude, inconsiderate person woke her up, in which case, she was decidedly testy. She inhaled slowly and threw open the window.

"What on earth do you think you're..." Kati stopped abruptly. Standing below, bold as brass was Luke, and he *was* throwing pebbles at her window. Her heart dragged, and then accelerated rapidly. He was dressed in gray slacks and a knit pullover that caressed his masculine frame. The early morning breeze ruffled his dark hair, causing it to spill boyishly over his forehead. His face lit up when he saw her.

"Good morning, Kati Rose," he called gaily, waving. "And how are you this fine Sunday morning?"

She looked at him like he was crazy, which at the moment, she was certain he was! What on earth was Luke doing here, she wondered, and at this hour?

"Are you out of your mind?" she asked, shoving a wad of hair out of her face in order to see him better and trying not to smile.

"Not that I know of," he said, cocking his head to see her better. "How are you?" he repeated again, and Kati looked at him wildly, trying not to soften at the look on his face. How on earth could this man look so good, and be so charming at this hour?

"Tired," she yelled down, shutting the window firmly and returning to bed. Lucas Kane was the kind of man to confront his feelings head-on. And Kati was still trying to run from hers, she realized, as she snuggled deeper beneath the covers. But how much longer could she keep on running?

In spite of herself Kati found a smile curve her lips. Early or not, crazy or not, even at this hour, the man was hard to ignore.

Luke started pelting the window again. Sighing tiredly, Kati tossed the covers off again. Obviously the man wasn't going to go away, and she wasn't going to get any more sleep this morning. Taking a deep breath, she

stomped across the room and threw the window open
again.

"Lucas Kane!" she yelled. "I don't know what you
think you're doing at this hour but— Oh my God," she
whimpered. Luke was still downstairs, but he wasn't
alone. Reverend Powers was standing right beside him!
Kati moaned softly. She was hanging out the window,
dressed only in her nightshirt, screeching like a barnyard
chicken! And Reverend Powers was standing below, listening to every word! She was going to strangle Lucas
Kane when she got her hands on him!

"Good morning, Kati Rose," Reverend Powers caroled gaily. His faint Irish accent drifted on the early
morning breeze. He looked up at her and waved, obviously delighted to see her.

"Good morning," she said weakly, wishing she could
crawl under her bed. Slowly, she inched backward, trying
to hide. She wasn't even dressed, for goodness' sakes!

"Isn't it a fine morning, Kati Rose?" the Reverend
asked and Kati took a deep, controlled breath. How on
earth did she get into this mess? Kati wondered if her
arms were long enough to reach Luke's neck from here.

"Yes, it is," she muttered, scowling as Luke grinned
from ear to ear.

"Lucas here tells me he's come to court you," the
Reverend told her, clearly delighted.

"He what?" Kati leaned out the window to glare at
Luke and then remembering her attire, quickly pulled her
head back inside. What kind of tales had Luke been telling the reverend? Didn't the man know you weren't supposed to tell fibs? Particularly—no, especially—to a man
of the cloth?

"I think it's a fine, old-fashioned idea, don't you, Kati
Rose?"

"Wonderful," she muttered, sending Luke cryptic messages with her eyes, and wondering what on earth she had ever done to deserve this. Public humiliation was not high on her list of things to do on Sunday morning.

"Well, I've got to be going now," Reverend Powers said, looking from Luke to Kati. "You two have fun." With a jaunty wave, he was off, leaving Kati to deal with Luke.

"Luke!" she cried, forgetting about her state of undress and leaning farther out the window. "What on earth did you tell Reverend Powers?"

"The truth," Luke called, clearly unperturbed by her anger.

"What do you mean the truth?" she hissed, trying to keep her voice down. Half the town was coming home from Sunday services and she certainly didn't want everyone to know her business.

Luke stepped closer, and cupped his hands over his mouth. "I told him I've come to court you." He attempted to whisper, but his deep voice carried well and came off just short of a shout. Kati winced, trying hard not to be charmed.

"Oh my word," Kati muttered, glancing up and down the street and heaving a sigh of relief. At least no one was within earshot. She hoped. "Will you stop that?"

"Stop what?" he asked, grinning.

"What do you want?" she asked, nearly falling out the window at the suggestive look he gave her. *She* knew what he wanted. *Her*. She just didn't want the whole town to know it! "Never mind," she hissed, deciding to change her tactics. "What are you doing here?"

Luke rocked back on his heels, crossing his arms over his chest. "I already told you what I'm doing here. If you didn't hear me, I could yell it a little louder,'' he threatened, clearly delighted at the look that crossed her face.

"Don't you dare,'' she cried, glancing quickly up and down the street.

"I've come to court you, Kati Rose,'' he called, and she had a feeling he fully intended to stand there shouting his intentions until she acknowledged him. Or died of embarrassment, whichever came first! He took a step closer and tilted his head back further. The sun glanced off the dark, damp strands of his hair, sending a glistening prism of light across the blue-black color. "Remember MayBelle?'' he inquired, cupping his hands over his mouth so that his voice carried better. Kati winced. With the husky baritone of his voice, no doubt everyone in this town and the next could hear him. "You did promise to help me out with that little problem, remember?''

Kati nodded, and waited for him to continue. She had a feeling this was going to be a long, drawn-out, perfectly logical explanation that was made up entirely of baloney. Lucas Kane knew very well that after all the help he had given her the past few weeks, she wouldn't have the heart to turn him down when he asked her for help. No matter what the problem. The little devil was going to play on her sympathies, she realized, feeling more charmed by the minute.

"What does MayBelle Watson have to do with you being here at the crack of dawn?'' she inquired with a questioning lift of her brow.

"Well, she asked me to go to Libertyville Lake with her on a picnic today.''

"And?'' Kati prompted, realizing he was going to take the long route around this explanation.

"I told her I couldn't go with her,'' he explained with a mischievous grin, rocking back on his heels and looking quite pleased with himself. "Because I was going with you."

"What?" she cried, forgetting about her state of undress and leaning out the window again.

"Kati, now listen. We're partners, and partners are supposed to help each other out of jams. Right?" He didn't wait for her to answer, but continued spinning his yarn. "How am I supposed to work if MayBelle's chasing me around the tables? Bad for our image," he concluded, his smile brightening. "Very bad. So you can see why it's necessary for you to go to the lake with me. Why, if I showed up there without you, MayBelle's feelings would be hurt. Devastated maybe." Grinning from ear to ear, Luke looked quite pleased with himself and Kati couldn't help but smile. The man had very strange ways of asking for a date. And she knew that's exactly what he was asking.

"Lucas Kane, what on earth am I going to do with you?" she inquired, laughing and shaking her head.

His brows rose suggestively and she shook her finger at him.

"Don't say it!" she cautioned, holding a hand up and sighing deeply. "Please?" She had to give the man an A for ingenuity and initiative.

"Are you coming down, or do I have to come up?" he called, making no attempt to lower his voice.

"Luke," she protested with a laugh, "I'm not even dressed yet!"

His grin widened. "Then I'm definitely coming up."

"No, you're not!" she said in a panic, glancing down at her ragged football jersey. She had no doubt that any man who would throw pebbles at her window, confess his intentions openly to the Reverend Powers in broad daylight, and weave tall tales in a single breath, would have no hesitancy in coming up whether she was dressed or not. "I'll come down," she assured him.

One brow rose. "How long?"

"Twenty minutes?"

"Ten," he countered with a playful smile.

"Fifteen?"

"Deal." Luke grinned again. "Fifteen minutes, then I'm coming up."

"All right. All right." She turned from the window, anxious to get dressed. Luke hadn't seen her in anything but her tattered jeans and white blouses she wore for work. Her femininity was crying to be let loose, and today seemed like a perfect day.

"Kati Rose?" Luke called, stopping her in her tracks. She turned back to the window, feeling a little thrill at the sight of him.

"Now what?" She had no idea what the day would hold, but she had decided she wanted—no, she needed—to find out just what there was between her and Luke, besides the diner. She was so unskilled in these man-woman things that she didn't know quite how to behave. When other young women were going through the dating rituals, she had been busy raising her brother and running a diner. It was time, Kati admitted, that she find out just what she'd been missing.

"You've only got fourteen minutes left," he warned, tapping his watch. "Better hurry."

And hurry she did. Anticipation caused her heart to soar and her feet to move—rapidly. She refused to be frightened by the excitement within her.

Kati suddenly realized that she had been wrong about Luke, dead wrong. He was her partner, deserved to be, he'd proven that. Now, Kati knew she wanted a chance to explore all the other things that were going on between them, all the things that had nothing to do with business. He had systematically charmed and knocked down every barrier she'd tried to erect. Maybe it was time for her to stop running, from herself, and from him.

Exactly fourteen-and-a-half minutes later, showered, dressed, and a bit out of breath, Kati raced out into the warm summer morning.

"Luke?" she called, looking around and blinking against the morning sunlight. He was nowhere to be found. "Luke?"

He came dashing around the corner, hiding something behind his back. Skidding to a stop in front of her, his eyes slowly took her in. He was looking at her intently, his beautiful blue eyes taking in the soft knit sweater that fit the contour of her curves like a second skin, sliding down the linen slacks that emphasized her narrow waist and long legs. His eyes slid back upward, slowly caressing everywhere he touched.

Wondering if she looked all right and nervous at his frank appraisal, Kati lifted a hand to self-consciously touch her hair which she had pulled back and secured with a tortoiseshell barrette. From the appreciative glint in Luke's eyes, Kati felt that he approved.

"Don't." He reached out and caught her hand in his, gently giving her an encouraging squeeze. The look of longing in his eyes nearly took her breath away. "You look beautiful," he whispered, and her heart fluttered wildly.

"Thank you," she returned, feeling suddenly shy with him.

Lacing his hand through hers, he started guiding her down the street, making no attempt to show her what he was hiding behind his back. Her curiosity suddenly grew.

"What are you hiding back there?" she asked, coming to an abrupt halt and trying to peek behind him. Luke dipped and ducked so she couldn't see.

"It's a surprise," he said mysteriously, taking her arm again.

"For me?" She laughed. "I'd say you were full of surprises this morning."

Luke came to an abrupt halt and turned to her. Lifting one hand, he gently caressed her cheek. His gaze held hers, a warm smile on his face. "These," he said tenderly, bringing his arm out from behind him, "are for you." Kati gasped as Luke presented her with a large bouquet of wildflowers.

She lifted her gaze to his and her pulse hammered foolishly. "Oh, Luke," she whispered, touched beyond measure. "They're beautiful."

A lopsided grin curved his lips. "I take my courting seriously, Kati Rose. And we have to make it look official, for MayBelle's sake," he added, trying to contain his smile, but failing miserably.

"For MayBelle's sake, of course." Kati lifted the bouquet and inhaled deeply, savoring the intoxicating scent. Twenty-seven years old and she'd never had a man give her flowers before. Her breath caught. These were all the more special because they were from Luke.

"Thank you." Standing on tiptoe, she planted a kiss on his cheek, holding the flowers close to her pounding heart.

"You're welcome. But your kiss missed its target." He pointed to his lips expectantly. "We have to make this look good," he insisted, sliding an arm around her shoulder and hauling her unsuspecting body close. On tiptoe again, Kati brushed her lips gently against his. His mouth covered hers, his lips hungry. Immediately, she responded to the call of his touch, lifting one arm to lace around his neck, and carefully protecting her precious flowers with the other. His sweet scent infiltrated her breathing space and she reeled with a rush of desire.

Groaning softly, Luke pulled away regretfully. "Kati Rose," he murmured, his voice husky. "If we don't stop this, *courting* won't be the only thing on my mind." His words brought a rush of color to her face and she took a step back.

"Now," he said, taking her hand and lacing his fingers through hers. "Vera said Libertyville Lake is only a few blocks from here. Do we walk, or take the truck?"

"The truck?" One auburn brow rose in inquiry. "You make it sound like it's the ultimate vehicle."

"It is, Kati. It is." He guided her to the curb where a brown pickup was parked. "This here's Sylvania," he declared proudly, giving the truck a friendly pat.

"Sylvania?" Kati inquired with a raised brow, examining the truck carefully. She didn't see anything particularly special about the truck except for its obvious ugliness. The paint, although she guessed it was supposed to be brown, was chipped and rusted in places. Splattered mud dulled what paint was visible. In the back bed lay several odd construction tools and a dusty blanket.

Stenciled on the side door were the words, *Kane Construction, Kansas City, Mo.* Kati frowned as she read the words.

"Luke, do you own a construction firm?" She lifted her eyes to his in question. He gave her a moment to examine the truck more closely before he answered.

"I'm not the owner of a construction company—anymore." He opened the door and helped her in. Surprisingly, the inside of the truck, in direct contrast to the

outside, was immaculate. Carefully, she placed her
flowers on the seat next to her. "I'm the owner of a diner.
Well, part owner at least," he corrected, climbing behind the wheel.

Kati looked at him, intrigued. She really didn't know
anything about Lucas Kane or his life before he came to
the diner, and she longed to know everything about this
wonderful, fascinating man. "Did you sell your company?" she asked, as he started the car and pulled onto
the empty street.

Luke nodded, turning down the street where she told
him. "I was burned out, I guess." He shrugged. "After
Leonard died, I kind of lost my desire to keep the business going. I didn't want the hassle anymore. I just
wanted out. I couldn't stand big business anymore."
Luke shrugged, his shoulders moving against the knit
shirt. "My heart just wasn't in it." He turned his head,
and his eyes pinned hers. "I guess I was looking for
something. I didn't know what it was until I met you."
His husky words caused her stomach to drop and she
struggled to ignore the implication, trying to pick up the
thread of Luke's conversation, as he continued.

"Anyway, I worked out a deal with my head foreman.
He didn't have the money to buy me outright, so he took
over the company, or at least the day-to-day running of
it, until a suitable buyer could be found, or until I decide what I'm going to do with it. That's how I met Patrick," he continued, glancing over at her. "He came to
work for me. What's wrong, Kati?" he asked, noticing
her sudden frown.

Kati twisted her hands nervously in her lap, her palms
suddenly warm. She hadn't realized Luke had even
owned a construction company, or anything else for that
matter. The thought that he had another business that

might possibly be waiting for his return brought on a sudden bout of suspicion. Why would a man up and leave his company, his friends, and family to claim half-ownership of a small-town diner? she wondered. It just didn't make sense.

She had tried so hard for so long to get rid of Luke, that now, when she'd finally accepted him as part of her life, when *she wanted* him to stay, just the thought that he might *not* be staying made her feel a bit of panic. At this moment, she couldn't imagine her life, either in or out of the diner, without him. He had so entangled himself in her daily life and in her every thought, that at times, she didn't know where her life stopped, and his began. He had sailed through her life as quickly and easily as wind whirled through a fence. Just the thought that he might not be staying made her nervous. And a bit suspicious.

"Who's Leonard?" she asked out loud. And what about the diner? she asked silently, trying to bank down the fear that tightened her heart.

Luke's face changed, not much, but enough for Kati to know that whoever the man was, he obviously was someone very important to Luke. Pulling the car into the beach lot, Luke parked, and turned off the motor.

"Leonard was—" Luke stopped to glance out the window. She could feel the sudden tension in him. "Leonard was my father...of sorts—" he said, choosing his words carefully. "Not my real father," he corrected quickly. "But that never mattered. He was more of a father to me than any real father could have been." He turned and flashed her a smile, but it didn't quite reach his eyes. There was that forlorn look in Luke's eyes again, she thought, feeling a tug at her heart.

"Were you adopted?"

Luke shook his head, not looking at her. "No, not officially. I was about sixteen and running away from the latest foster home when I met Leonard. I broke into one of his construction trailers one night, looking for a warm place to sleep." He laughed softly, but the sound was riddled with pain. "I didn't know it at the time, but that probably was the smartest thing I ever did. Until I met you," he added tenderly, reaching out to caress her hand. "It was Leonard's trailer, and he was in there sleeping on a couch when I broke in. Boy, I don't know who was more scared, him or me." Luke laughed softly. "He almost boxed my ears that first night, but when he realized I was all alone like him, something clicked between us. Two souls, all alone and lonely." Kati squeezed his hand, feeling a deep-seated ache for the troubled boy Luke must have been.

"Leonard was wonderful," he continued, looking out the window. "He took me in, and straightened me out. Treated me like a son. He made me go to school, gave me a job, and taught me to be a man. It was the first real home I'd ever had. He gave me something else I thought I'd never have." Luke jammed a hand through his hair and sighed heavily.

"What?" she asked cautiously, longing to know everything about Luke, and his life.

"His name," he said quietly, and Kati could feel the tension seep out of him.

"His name?" she whispered, clearly not understanding him. "But what about your parents? Your family?"

"Guess they didn't want me," he said, and Kati watched a wall of hurt slowly unfold and surround him. "My dad ran off and left my ma when she was expecting me. She was young and couldn't take care of a baby, so she just left me at the hospital. They weren't equipped to deal with a newborn. So they turned me over to an orphanage. They didn't know what to call me, so they named me John Smith. Original, don't you think?'' Luke laughed harshly, and Kati winced at the pain that was still so vivid in the man. ''I lived in a series of foster homes until I was old enough to start running away. I guess I was just running from myself,'' he said softly, the hurt still evident in the harsh raggedness of his voice.

Kati's eyes slid closed in remorse as she remembered the night Luke had arrived at the diner. The night she told him *she* didn't want him here. *It won't be the first time I've not been wanted,* he had told her then, and now she understood. Kati swallowed hard around the sudden lump in her throat. Her heart ached, and she longed to wipe away all Luke's sad memories, all the years without love—and all the days that she herself, out of blind stubborn pride had inflicted more hurt, more pain. Luke knew she hadn't wanted him. She couldn't have made it plainer. Remorse swept over her. How could she have been so stupid? So cruel?

When she thought about her own happy childhood, at least before her parents' untimely death, she could imagine how hard it had been for Luke. Guilt burned through her at the way she had treated him. He'd been nothing but kind to her. Oh, he drove her crazy, constantly underfoot and on her mind, charming, disarming and storming her vulnerable heart until she was certain she would faint. But that certainly didn't excuse the way she had been treating him.

''Leonard Kane was a rare man,'' Luke said softly, draping an arm around her. Kati snuggled close to him. Her fingers clutched tightly to the material of his shirt.

She shifted her face and looked up at him, her heart full of love. Lucas Kane was also a rare man. After all he

had been through, other than the last few moments, Kati
had never sensed the bitterness, the hurt he must have
felt.

"Oh, Luke," she whispered, knowing that no matter
how hard or how fast she ran, no matter how many bar-
riers she threw up, no matter how she lied or tried to deny
it, she couldn't ignore what she felt for this man. Lord,
somehow when she wasn't looking, this interfering in-
terloper had stolen more than her diner. Luke had stolen
her heart, as well.

"Kati," he murmured, bending to claim her waiting
mouth. Teasing her with his tenderness, Kati slid her
arms around him and leaned against him. She could feel
the hard muscular length of his thighs against the thin
material of her slacks. Feel the rapid beat of his heart
against the crush of her breasts.

All too soon he pulled away, but Kati didn't move. She
stayed snuggled against him, wanting only to feel the
warmth he offered.

"Now, Kati Rose Ryan," he said finally, all traces of
sadness gone from him. "It's time to start some serious
courting, here." Smiling, he popped open his door and
hopped out. She slid over to her own side of the car and
started to open the door, but he reached out his hand to
slap hers away. "Kati Rose," he scolded. "A courting
gentleman always opens a door for a lady." Bowing gallantly, in much the same way he had done to Vera, Luke
opened her door and extended his hand to help her out.
Reaching in the back of the cab, Luke extracted a picnic
basket from under a blanket. With their arms around
each other, they walked toward the sandy beach.

Although early, the warmth of the day had brought out
a lot of people. Tiptoeing over blankets and dodging
toddlers making sand castles, they found a spot on a

small ridge. Kati watched in surprise as Luke pulled out a blanket and a thermos of coffee.

"You certainly came prepared," she teased, folding her legs under her and sitting Indian style on the blanket. "What else have you got in there?" she inquired, trying to peek.

"You'll see," he admonished, gently slapping her hand away. "Now, tell me about Kati Rose Ryan." Luke poured them each a cup of coffee, and handed one to her before stretching his lean frame alongside of her and resting his head in her lap. She glanced down at him. She felt so comfortable with him, so relaxed, so at peace.

"There's not much to tell," she admitted, suddenly realizing how boring her life had been. Until she'd met Luke. "I was born and raised in Libertyville, and have never even thought of leaving." She glanced around at the familiar surroundings. "This is home. My parents were killed when Patrick was still rather young. I had a normal childhood, until then." Her voice dropped an octave as memories overwhelmed her. Talking about her parents was still hard, even after all this time. "I took the little bit of insurance money they left and bought the diner. It was a way to support myself and Patrick. I sold the house, and we moved to the apartment upstairs." She took a sip of her coffee, aware that Luke's eyes were watching her intently.

"What about boyfriends?" he asked, and Kati laughed shortly, grateful to change the subject.

"I was too busy raising my brother and trying to keep the diner afloat."

"Come on, Kati," he teased, lifting a hand to stroke her cheek. "Don't tell me you never had a serious relationship? No old flames lurking in the background with a broken heart?"

"Well, there was Eddie Fredricks—"

"Aha, the plot thickens. Tell me about poor Eddie," he said, clearly enjoying himself. "I'll bet you broke his heart, didn't you?"

Kati gave him a mysterious grin, deciding to play him along for a while. "I guess I did. Poor Eddie." She sighed expressively, struggling not to laugh. "He was an older man," she confessed, the smile winning out. "He was in third grade, and I was in first. He used to walk me home from school every day. One day he cornered me behind the old lilac bush in front of Vera's and tried to kiss me."

"And?" Luke prompted, lifting one brow.

"And I popped him one right in the kisser," she admitted, delighted at the whoop of laughter that shook Luke's frame. "I broke his glasses."

"And Eddie?"

She laughed softly. "Eddie wore adhesive tape between his eyes for the rest of the year, and I had to carry my own books home from that day on. I don't know why, but Eddie never tried to kiss me again."

"Poor Eddie," Luke said, taking her empty cup from her hand and pulling her down beside him. "He should have hung in there. A kiss from you would be worth a pop in the nose any day." He leaned forward, planting a soft kiss on her mouth. He drew back, his eyes searching her face. "What about now, Kati?" he asked, his voice light. But she sensed the significance of his question. "Any boyfriends?"

It was a strange question to ask, particularly now, Kati thought wryly. If Luke was truly courting her, it might have been a good idea to find out about her boyfriend situation before this.

She shook her head. "No," she said simply, glancing away from him to stare at the glistening blue water of the lake. The water lapped gently against the shore, bringing a warm, wet breeze against her skin.

"Why not?" he asked, pressing the issue. Kati sighed. This was delicate territory, and a bit hard for her to discuss.

"I guess I just haven't had the time," she said, not quite truthfully. She looked at him and knew he hadn't really believed her. He had talked so openly and honestly about himself, it was only fair that she do the same. "That's not quite the truth," she admitted, meeting his gaze. "After my parents died, I had a bit of a hard time. I went from a carefree teenager with no responsibility, to a full-fledged adult left with a young boy to raise. I had relied on my parents for everything. It was a shock to suddenly find myself responsible not only for my own well-being, but my brother's as well. I was so scared," she whispered, remembering all the days that had followed her parents' death and the stark fear that had haunted her. "I had no one to lean on, no one to depend on but myself. It was so hard," she whispered, blinking back sudden tears. "I had to learn fast. Patrick was depending on me. I had no choice but to grow up quickly. Independence was so hard to come by, but once I had it, I worked hard at it. I didn't ever want to rely on someone again, to need them and then—" Kati tried to smile against a spurt of tears that seemed to come from nowhere.

"And then to be left alone," Luke said, understanding completely. "So that's why your independence is so important." It was a statement not a question, and she nodded. Luke lifted her hand and kissed it reassuringly, and she looked at him, touched by the look of anguish reflected in his eyes.

"It seemed like the best way for me. I had the diner and Patrick, but then..." Her voice faltered a bit. "Then Patrick left and I had to learn all over again."

Luke swore softly, and Kati smiled. It was the first time she had ever heard him say anything of that kind.

"You miss him, don't you?" Luke asked, wishing he could thrash Patrick Ryan for his immature nature. And for hurting Kati. No wonder she was so skittish and fearful. No wonder she never wanted to need anyone or lean on anyone. To her, hurt and need were one and the same.

"Yes," she admitted. "I miss him, but I don't need him anymore," she said fiercely. "Not like before."

"And now?"

She glanced down at him, knowing what he was asking, but not certain she could give him an answer. "Now?"

"Do you need anyone now?" There was no mistaking the question this time. Luke wasn't talking about Patrick, or the diner, or anything else but him and her.

"I don't know," she answered, as a bit of the fear returned. It wasn't the truth. She needed Luke, but she didn't know if she was ready to admit that to him.

"Well, I do, Kati," Luke whispered. "Needing someone doesn't mean giving up your independence, or asking for heartache. It just means sharing your life, and your love. You scare me, Kati Rose Ryan," Luke said suddenly, his eyes snaring hers.

"Me?" she declared, clearly shocked. "Why on earth do I scare you?"

He looked at her long and hard. "Because it seems my whole life I was lost until I met Leonard. After he died, I felt all the old feelings again. Then I met you, and the moment I did..." His voice trailed off and Luke lifted a hand to caress her cheek, his fingers warm and tender against her skin. "I feel at peace here. I finally feel like I'm home. I need you, Kati," he whispered softly, running a finger across her lips. "And you need me. What I feel for you doesn't have anything to do with the diner."

"I know," she whispered, nestling her cheek against the warmth of his hand. She knew what Luke was saying, knew what he was asking. What she *didn't* know was if she could handle it. What she felt for Luke had nothing to do with the diner, either. What she felt for Luke was something more, much more, and it frightened her. Kati didn't know if she ever wanted to need anyone again. She'd been all alone so long, she didn't realize she'd been missing anything. Until now.

"Don't worry, Kati," he said, sensing her fear. "I'm not Eddie, I'm not going to turn tail and bolt, even if you do pop me in the kisser." His words made her smile. "I'm made of heartier stuff than that. I can be patient, let you get used to the idea. But, Kati, I want you to know, I intend to share a whole lot more than the diner with you." His words caused her pulse to flutter wildly. She wanted—no, needed—to share a whole lot more than the diner with him, but she was scared.

Luke slid his fingers into a wispy curl at her temple and gently caressed the silky auburn strand. A sense of contentment stole through her at the look on his face.

"My sweet Kati Rose," he purred, sliding his fingers to the nape of her neck and sending a tingling shiver through the length of her. Sensing her fear, Luke decided to change the subject, reminding himself to go slow. "Now, are you ready for the second phase of this courtship?" he asked mischievously, pulling himself into a sitting position.

"What? There's more? First flowers, then coffee. What's next?"

Grinning crookedly, Luke pulled the picnic basket closer and opened the top. Kati tried to peek over the lid, but he protected it with his arm, not letting her see. "No peeking," he scolded, wagging a finger at her. "Now, close your eyes," he instructed, and she did what she was told. For a second. Squinting, she opened one eye a fraction, but he caught her.

"Kati Rose," he admonished, trying unsuccessfully to give her a stern look. "I saw that beautiful emerald eye open. Now close your eyes or you won't get your present," he threatened.

"Another present?" She laughed and closed her eyes properly this time. She felt Luke's breath on her face a moment before his lips touched hers. Sighing, she slid her arms around his neck. "You tricked me," she murmured against his mouth, and felt his lips turn upward beneath hers.

"I know." Luke slid his lips from hers, and she opened her eyes. He was holding a sugar jelly doughnut just out of her reach.

"How did you know?" she asked gleefully, appreciatively eyeing her favorite pastry.

"Oh, a little bird told me," he murmured mysteriously.

"More like a big waitress," she recanted, diving forward and trying to catch her treat. Bessie was the only one who knew about her penchant for these particular doughnuts.

Luke laughed softly. "One jelly doughnut for a kiss. It's only fair, Kati. You give me something, and I'll give you something."

"I'll give you something," she threatened, diving forward and landing squarely on top of him. Luke threw his legs around hers, trapping her on top of him. Her body immediately responded to his, arching and aching with a sweet tenderness that left her slightly breathless. A pulsing throb raced the length of her, coiling her nerves into knots as his languid gaze slid over her. Perhaps, she realized a bit belatedly, a kiss would have been simpler.

His eyes stroked her face, and she returned his gaze, allowing her eyes to caress the now familiar features. The dark brows that rose with mischief, or gathered with annoyance. The glistening blue eyes that seemed to see and touch her very soul. The slightly crooked nose that had never seemed quite so wonderful. The full mouth that her own lips ached to claim. And did.

The doughnut forgotten, Luke slid his arms around her waist, settling her more comfortably to fit his body. His hands slid down the curve of her hips, pulling her closer. She was lost in a wave of pleasure, oblivious to anything but Luke.

"Kati Rose! My dear, what are you doing to Luke?" The high pitched shrill of Vera's voice broke through the sensuous web surrounding Kati. Lifting her head, Kati turned her startled gaze to Vera. Hands on hips, the woman, dressed in her ever-present suit, hat and gloves was glaring at Kati like a mother cub protecting her young.

Embarrassed, Kati jumped to her feet, trying in vain to smooth the wisps of hair that had come loose from her barrette. Of all times for Vera to show up!

"I—I—" Kati stammered, and looked helplessly at Luke. How on earth could she explain exactly what she'd been doing to Luke? And him! He was grinning from ear to ear, and obviously enjoying himself. She scowled at him.

"Vera," Luke said, hauling himself to a standing position and plowing a hand through his hair in an effort to straighten it. "What brings you to Libertyville Lake?" he asked, trying not to grin at Kati who stood perfectly still in mortification. Vera glanced fitfully at Kati who blushed scarlet.

Clearing her throat, Vera tried to regain her composure. "I was looking for Mr. Billings. He was supposed to meet me here. We're going on a picnic," she explained hurriedly at the look of astonishment on Kati's face.

Vera and Mr. Billings couldn't get along for two minutes in the same room. Good Lord, why on earth would they want to spend the afternoon together?

"Are you all right, dear?" Vera asked, bending down to inspect Luke for any damage and throwing an accusing glance at Kati. Ducking her head, Kati tried to hide her smile.

"I'm fine," Luke laughed, leaning forward to give Vera a hug. Flustered at his obvious display of affection, Vera straightened her hat.

"Are you sure, dear?" she asked worriedly and Luke laughed again.

"I'm sure. There's Mr. Billings," Luke announced, pointing. All eyes turned down the beach to watch Mr. Billings and Beauregard approach.

"Now why on earth would that man bring that rodent with him?" Vera huffed, jamming her hands on her hips. "I don't know why he has to take that dog everywhere." She turned to Luke, a frown causing her hat to dip haphazardly over her forehead. "It's unsavory, you know. He's more attached to that animal than he is to—" Her lips snapped shut and Kati and Luke exchanged curious glances. "Well, dear, I'd better go let him know where I am." She leaned over and pecked Luke on the cheek. "You take care now, you hear?" Vera frowned suddenly, deep in thought. "Perhaps you'd like us to leave Beauregard with you? He's very good for *protection*," Vera said, leaving little doubt as to *who* she thought needed protection from *whom*. Kati ducked her head to hide a smile, but Vera caught her.

"Kati Rose?"

"Yes?" Kati said, trying not to laugh, and resisting the urge to slap her hand to her forehead in a mock salute.

"You take care of my Luke here," she instructed sternly. "He's a wonderful boy, and I wouldn't want anything to happen to him." With that, Vera turned on her high heels and ambled off through the sand while trying to maintain her dignity, shoving her hat back in place every few minutes.

Laughing, Kati and Luke collapsed against each other. "This was all your fault," she accused, poking a finger into his midsection. "It was your idea of trading a kiss for a doughnut! She thinks I was assaulting you!"

"Hey," he protested, draping an arm around Kati's neck, and dragging her close. "You'd better be careful," he threatened gleefully, wagging a finger at her. "I might tell Vera on you."

"Oh, yeah!" Her fingers hit his ticklish middle, and laughing wildly, Luke tumbled to the ground pulling her down with him.

"Oh, no, you don't," she protested, trying to squirm off of him. "This is how I got into trouble in the first place. If Vera comes back—" He kissed her quick to stop the flow of words. Laughing, Kati looked right into his eyes, feeling giddy all of a sudden. She felt comfortable and relaxed for the first time in weeks, and she knew Lucas Kane was the reason.

"You heard Vera," Luke whispered, nibbling at her ear. "You're supposed to take care of me. *I'm* wonderful, remember?" he teased.

Kati sighed dreamily. "I know," she whispered softly, sliding her arms around his neck. "I know."

Chapter Eight

"Good morning, Kati Rose." Coming up behind her, Luke slid his arms around her and gave her a resounding kiss on her cheek. "Well, at least it's good now," he murmured, dipping his lips to the soft warmth of her neck.

"Good morning, yourself," Kati replied, turning her head to capture his mouth. Since Sunday, their relationship had taken on a new dimension. There was a playfulness, a warmth that seemed to bind her to Luke. She could no longer deny she was falling in love with him.

The air arced with so much tension when he was anywhere near her that Kati feared Bessie, who had recovered from her flu and returned earlier in the week, could sense it. Not much went on that Bessie didn't know about. If she suspected anything, she never said a word. But Kati had caught Bessie looking at her strangely once or twice. Kati tried to hide her feelings for Luke, but it was hard. She had never been quite so happy before.

"Kati?" Luke looked at the assembled food on the counter. "Aren't you getting carried away a bit?" He plucked a sandwich off the tray she was preparing and eyed it hungrily. She snatched it out of his hands and returned it to the tray.

"Those sandwiches are for tonight. Don't touch," she scolded as he reached for another sandwich. His hands stopped midway to the tray and he looked at her with a frown.

"Tonight?" He was looking at her with such confusion, she laughed.

"Luke, tonight is the fourth Saturday of the month."

One brow rose skeptically. "That's an interesting bit of information," he said dryly, trying without success to contain a crooked smile. "Do you suppose you could tell me what that has to do with anything? These sandwiches in particular?"

"Don't you remember?" she asked, realizing once the words were out that obviously Luke didn't remember, or he wouldn't be asking. "The fourth Saturday of the month is the Village Hall dance. We cater the food, remember?" She had told him all about the dance at the beginning of the week.

A light of recognition dawned in his blue eyes, and he slapped a hand to his forehead. "Of course, I completely forgot. What time do I have to be there?"

Kati glanced at him strangely, his words echoing in her mind. What time did *he* have to be there? She just assumed they would be going together. "The dance starts at seven," she said a bit stiffly, wondering if her assumptions had been wrong. "But generally I try to get there early to set the food and tables up. So if you come get me about five-thirty we'll have plenty of time."

"Do you think Bessie can help you with the food tonight?" he asked. "I have a date."

"A date!" The words came out before she could stop them. Anger and jealousy waged a war within her. Luke had a date for the dance and obviously he wasn't in the least bit concerned about admitting it to her! The idea of popping him one in the kisser was growing more appealing by the moment, she thought darkly. Refusing to give in to the emotions raging within, Kati lifted her chin stubbornly. If Luke had a date for the dance, fine. It was none of her concern, she thought darkly, knowing all the while it *was* her concern. She was furious at him and his insensitivity, and she was not willing to admit that Luke's admission hurt. And hurt deeply. She wasn't going to ask although she was dying to know. MayBelle Watson came immediately to mind.

"Now, Kati, don't tell me you're jealous?" he said boldly, admiring the fire that danced in her eyes.

"Me?" she declared airily. "Jealous?" She hacked at a loaf of bread. "Now why on earth would I be jealous?" she asked, trying hard to unclench her teeth. "You're perfectly free to date anyone you choose. We're business partners, remember?" Just saying the words caused her heart to ache. Luke was becoming so much more.

Luke's eyes darkened and for a moment she was certain he was going to say something. But he caught himself, and lifted a hand to ruffle her hair instead. Any other time she would have found the gesture endearing. Today, under the circumstances, it just made her mad. He was dating someone else and then he had the audacity to treat her like a little sister!

"Don't you have some work to do?" she inquired testily, determined not to let him know how she really felt.

"I guess I do." He headed for the door. "Oh, by the way, Kati. Save me a dance."

Save him a dance, indeed! He'd better be worried about saving his precious hide and not about her saving a dance for him, she thought darkly. It took all her willpower not to throw something at his retreating back. She wouldn't dance with Lucas Kane if he were the last man on earth! she decided, slapping the sandwiches together. And just to prove it, Kati picked up the phone and quickly dialed Wilfred's number, tapping her foot impatiently while she waited for him to come on the line.

"Wilfred, it's Kati Rose. Yes, I'm fine." She scowled and gave the wall a solid kick with the toe of her shoe when Wilfred inquired about Luke's health. "He's fine, too," she finally admitted through clenched teeth. "Wilfred, listen, the reason I'm calling is—do you have a date for the dance tonight? Bessie?" she repeated, her eyes widening in stunned surprise. This was a strange development, she thought, wondering how long Bessie and Wilfred had been dating. "No, I understand. No, please, don't worry about me. Wilfred, no, I certainly wouldn't want to tag along." She laughed softly. "You know what they say about three being a crowd. No, I'm fine, now don't worry about it. I'll see you tonight. Goodbye." Muttering under her breath Kati slammed down the phone just as a sharp knock sounded at the back door.

"Come in," she yelled. "The door's open." She turned just in time to see a deliveryman loaded down with boxes enter the kitchen.

"This Mabel's?" he asked, and Kati nodded, hurrying over to relieve him of the largest box. "Had a heck of a time finding this place. Sorry I'm so late."

Kati examined the brown cartons curiously. "What is this?" She had been using the same suppliers for years and knew most of the deliverymen by name. Both the supplies and the man were strangers to her.

"Potato chips," he said, huffing as he lowered the boxes to the floor. "Where do you want them?"

"Potato chips!" Kati frowned at him. "Well, why on earth are you bringing them here? Are you sure you've got the right place?"

Pulling a pad out of his back pocket, he flipped several sheets up. "Here it is. You Mabel?" he asked.

"No—yes. This is Mabel's. But I'm not Mabel," she explained into his suddenly dubious face.

"I see." He lifted his hat and scratched his head, clearly perplexed. Obviously he didn't see, but she was in no mood to go into a lengthy explanation of the diner's ownership history. "Look lady, I'm just the deliveryman. You call in the orders. I deliver. Now where do you want these boxes?"

"Are you sure they belong here?" she asked again, clearly confused.

"Lady." He sighed, and replaced his cap on his head. "Could you give me a break here? I've driven all the way from Rockford, Illinois, to deliver these chips, and I've got more stops to make. Could you just sign for these and tell me where to put them so I can get going?"

Kati looked at him, and then down at the cartons. "Yes, sure. I'm sorry." She took the pad he extended toward her and noticed Luke's name. She glanced up at the man, fury simmering through her. No wonder she didn't know anything about this delivery! Why on earth would Luke be ordering potato chips, or anything else for that matter? She handled all the supply orders. And if he was going to start changing suppliers, the least he could have done was discuss the matter with her. He had another date for the dance tonight, and now he was taking over her business and her chores!

"Could you wait just a moment?" she asked. "Please?" Crossing the kitchen before he had a chance to object, Kati pushed the door open. "Luke?" she called, trying to keep the anger out of her voice and not succeeding. Some of the old fear returned. "Luke! Could I see you in the kitchen for a moment?"

"What's up?" he asked, his face breaking into a wide smile when he saw the deliveryman. "It's about time. I was beginning to think they wouldn't get here. Just put those cartons in the pantry. Right through here," he instructed, hoisting a carton to his shoulder and leading the way.

Doing a slow simmer, Kati tapped her foot impatiently, trying to quell the resentment bubbling through her. "Luke, what is all this?" she asked, talking to his back as she followed him into the pantry.

"Chips," he said simply, dropping a quick kiss to her lips before pulling open one of the boxes.

"We already have a chip supplier," she protested, trying to ignore his kiss and maintain her anger. "We've been using the same chips for years."

"I know. That's part of the problem. The chips we use get stale quickly, and they really don't have much flavor."

"But Luke—" She caught the bag he tossed at her, glaring at the silver bag. "Mr. G's?" she read, one brow lifting in skepticism.

"Now, Kati, don't say anything until you try them. Taste."

Sighing, she tried to hand the bag back to him, but he tore it open and lifted a chip to her lips. "Luke—"

"Taste," he repeated, watching while she opened her mouth and chewed carefully. They were delicious. But she was too angry and too resentful to admit it, and her anger had little to do with suppliers or chips. It had more to do with the dance and Luke's date!

"Well?" he asked, waiting and watching her.

"That's it, folks." The deliveryman looked from one to the other, as if deciding which one should sign his pad. Flashing Kati a sympathetic smile, he handed the pad to Luke, bringing an immediate scowl to her face.

"If you wanted to change suppliers the least you could have done was discussed it with me!" she admonished, once the deliveryman had left.

"Are you mad at me, Kati Rose?" Luke asked mischievously, coming close to peer into her furious face.

"Mad!" She drew back, trying to bank the flames of her temper. "Now why on earth would I be—Stop that! Don't you dare kiss me when I'm mad!"

"I love it when you're mad, Kati Rose," Luke whispered against her mouth, not paying the least bit of attention to her directives and kissing her again. He reached down and plucked a chip from the bag and popped it into his mouth. "Don't forget, save me a dance." Whistling softly, Luke strode from the room.

Maybe she should have shot him when she had a chance, Kati thought glumly, glaring at the bag of chips.

If she hadn't spent so much time getting dressed—no, changing her clothes—she wouldn't be this late for the dance, Kati decided, hurrying to slash a bit of color on her mouth. Grabbing a bottle of perfume, she doused herself liberally, then fanned the air and tried to breathe without wheezing. Whew, that was strong stuff!

Kati had changed her clothes about a dozen times, finally deciding on a slinky black number that her brother Patrick had bought her for her birthday two years ago. She'd never worn the dress because it made her look like a seductive siren from the forties with its side slit to her thigh and its plunging low-cut neckline. But tonight, she decided a seductive siren was exactly what she wanted to look like. She was going to show Lucas Kane! A date, indeed! She had been simmering in her own anger all day just thinking about it. Kati slipped on her black high heels and raced from her apartment.

Bessie and Wilfred had already picked up the food from the diner, so Kati walked through the warm summer evening, trying to hurry in her high-heeled shoes. Finally in exasperation, she kicked her shoes off, hooked them over her thumb and hurried along in her bare feet.

The building the dance was held in was lit up like Christmas and Kati could hear the musicians warming up. She slipped in the back door, pausing to slide her feet back into her pumps.

"Where's Luke?" Bessie asked immediately when she spotted Kati all alone. "Did you two have another spat?" Her wise gray eyes shrewdly assessed Kati's.

"No, we didn't," she assured Bessie, making her way to the table where the food was set up. "Mr. Kane had a date."

"*Mr. Kane?* A date!" Bessie declared incredulously, as if Kati had just announced she'd joined the foreign legion.

Kati gave what she hoped was an indifferent shrug. "That's what the man said."

"What kind of a date?" Bessie hissed, leaning close to Kati so no one else could hear her.

"The usual kind, I assume," Kati retorted airily, shrugging her shoulders. "I really didn't ask him."

Bessie shook her gray head, her annoyance clearly evident. "It's your own fault, Kati Rose," she scolded, wagging a bent finger in Kati's direction. "You've been treating that boy like a flea-bitten mongrel ever since he arrived. And now he's off dating someone else. And what are you going to do about it?"

"Bessie!" Kati said, trying not to look past the woman to the gathering crowd to see if she could spot Luke. "I'm not going to do anything about it. If Luke wants to date someone else he has every right." *No he didn't,* her mind shouted. How could he do this to her? Bessie was right, Kati admitted sadly. It was her own fault if Luke was dating someone else. After the way she had treated him when he first arrived, she really couldn't blame him. But these past few weeks, she had thought their relationship had been repaired, and was now thriving. Apparently she was wrong.

"Every right, my foot," Bessie declared, not bothering to lower her voice this time. Kati winced as a group of men walked up to the table to help themselves to some sandwiches. Kati smiled at them and handed out plates, all the while knowing that Bessie was standing there scowling at her. Bessie waited until the men drifted off before continuing. "Kati Rose, now I know you don't like being told what to do."

"I'm glad you recognize that, Bessie," Kati said smoothly, trying not to smile. Bessie always told her what to do and meddled in her life whether it was her business or not. "I don't suppose you're going to tell me what to do, are you?" Kati asked, with an inquiring lift of her brow.

"Humph. Ain't never stopped me before," Bessie declared, placing her hands on her ample hips and causing Kati to chuckle softly. "Now you listen up, Kati Rose. Lucas Kane is the best thing to come to town since the new highway interchange. You're just too prideful and pigheaded to notice." She leaned across the table again. "Now I told you since the day he arrived, he's not like your brother's other friends. This one's different. And it's about time you started believing it. Unless you open those pretty green eyes of yours, you are going to lose that boy before you even have him." Bessie's eyes narrowed. "Men like Lucas Kane don't come along that often. And I don't think I need to tell you that he's crazy about you. Any *fool* could see it," Bessie declared firmly, leaving little doubt as to *who* she thought the fool was.

Kati sighed heavily and her heart ached a bit. Perhaps Bessie saw things that she didn't. If Luke was so crazy about her, why was he bringing someone else to the dance?

"You just think about what I said, Kati Rose," Bessie instructed before stomping off toward Wilfred. Kati glanced around the room. Most of the townspeople were there already. The monthly dance was the big social event of every month. She spotted his dark head at the opposite end of the room. He was hard to miss, for he stood head and shoulders above everyone else in the room. Her eyes followed him. She watched as he stopped and leaned down to talk to MayBelle Watson. Kati's temper flared. So MayBelle was his date! Obviously the woman had chased him long enough and hard enough, and now she'd finally caught him.

Kati glanced down at herself self-consciously. If she looked like a seductive siren when she left the house tonight, now, in contrast to the flaming red dress and elaborate hairdo MayBelle was sporting, Kati decided she looked more like a high school kid. No wonder Luke wanted to take MayBelle to the dance instead of her.

Luke headed in her direction and Kati pretended to be desperately interested in adjusting a plate of sandwiches that didn't need adjusting. He looked wonderful. His navy pin-striped suit was set off by a crisp, freshly starched white button-down shirt. His tie was a combination of blue and red that added to the look of sophistication. His black hair was still damp and curled boyishly across his forehead. She eyed him longingly, then quickly averted her gaze so he wouldn't catch her.

"Kati?" Luke did a double take when he got a close look at her dress. "That is some dress," he murmured, letting his eyes rove across her.

"Is it?" she returned flippantly, moving on to straighten the olives and pickles in an effort to keep her hands busy.

"It is," he confirmed, plucking her hands free of their busy work and holding them tightly in his. She knew she should yank free, but she was delighted to touch him, to have his attention, even if he did have another date.

"Where's MayBelle?" she asked, instantly regretting her words.

"MayBelle?" he asked with a lift of his brow. He glanced over his shoulder. "To tell you the truth, I really don't know." He looked back at her, his eyes intent on hers. "I don't really care."

"You don't?" she asked hopefully, wondering why he was dating someone he didn't even care about. The man was going to make her crazy!

"I don't," he confirmed, giving her hands a reassuring squeeze. "Have you seen my date anywhere?" he inquired, slipping one hand in the pocket of his slacks and looking entirely too pleased with himself.

Kati's lips pursed tightly together. If the man couldn't keep track of his date, what made him think *she* could?

"Here I am, Luke," Vera called gaily, waving a white handkerchief in the air. "My, Kati Rose, don't you look lovely this evening?" Vera's eyes sparkled brightly as she linked her arm through Luke's. "Wasn't it wonderful of Luke to escort me to the dance this evening? Mr. Billings was going to, but we had a bit of a falling-out yesterday. And I certainly didn't want to attend all alone. It wouldn't look right, you know, for a lady in my position," she said proudly, glancing affectionately at Luke. "So Luke offered to escort me." Luke patted her hand and smiled at the older woman. The affection between them was genuine, and Kati felt her heart fill with love for Luke. What a stinker he was! Making her think he had a real date!

"Yes, it was," Kati acknowledged, remembering what Bessie had told her earlier. Luke had made Vera one happy lady. And she added silently, he had made her very happy, too.

"Vera, I was wondering if you might mind the food table for a few moments," Luke asked, looking directly at Kati. "I promised Kati Rose here a dance."

"I'd be delighted," Vera said, unlinking her arm from Luke's, and coming behind the refreshment table to relieve Kati. "Now, you two young people enjoy yourselves," she said, shooing them away. "Take your time. Maybe Mr. Billings will drop by while you're gone," she whispered wistfully, scanning the crowd.

Luke held out his arm and guided Kati across the room toward the dance floor. His fingers were warm around her waist. A soft waltz was playing and she went willingly into Luke's arms.

"You think you're pretty cute, don't you?" Kati asked him finally, sliding both arms around Luke's neck and arching her body close to his. He gave her an entire afternoon of worry for nothing!

"Me? Cute?" Grinning, Luke lifted a hand and rubbed it across his cheek. "Well, thank you, Kati Rose, I didn't know you'd noticed." Oh, she'd noticed all right. And so had every other woman in town.

"Why didn't you tell me Vera was your date?" she inquired, drawing back her head so she could look at him. He was grinning crookedly.

"I don't believe you asked," he retorted innocently. "Why, if you would have asked, I surely would have told you."

She looked at him skeptically. Why did she get the feeling he had deliberately led her on, making her think he had a regular date? Had he tried to make her jealous on purpose?

"Were you jealous, Kati Rose?" he asked, his breath warm against her skin.

"Me?" She feigned shock, making her eyes wide as saucers, and trying not to grin guiltily.

"Yes, you, Kati Rose," Luke said knowingly, sliding his arm tighter around her and guiding her toward the door.

"Where are we going?" she asked, following him obediently. She saw Bessie watching them from across the room, an interesting smile on her face.

"Outside to talk," he said firmly, pushing open the back door with his arm.

"Can't we talk inside?" she asked, trying to adjust her eyes to the evening darkness. The sky was pitch black, the only light a sparkling of moonlight and a flash of stars that twinkled majestically across the soft darkness. Luke backed her up against the wall, his handsome features bathed in the soft glow of the moon.

"What I've got to say and what you've got to say is better said in private. Out here." The huskiness of his words caused her senses to spiral.

"Here?" she repeated weakly as Luke moved even closer. She could see the glint of desire darken his eyes and her breathing grew shallow.

"Here," Luke insisted, his voice deep and trembling as he slid his arms around her waist. The evening breeze was warm against her face, tumbling her hair into a tangled mass. Luke reached out and pushed the hair from her face. "Now, admit it, you were jealous, weren't you?"

"I was not—" His lips silenced hers, sending shivers of desire racing through her. Her breathing grew ragged, and she leaned into him, sliding her arms around his neck and pulling him even closer.

"You were saying?" he prompted softly, teasing one corner of her mouth with his intoxicating tongue. Shivers of feminine awareness screamed to life, and she sagged against Luke, savoring the hard masculine feel of him.

"Jealous," she murmured, the words more air than sound, as his tongue found hers again. Her breathing grew light and ragged as he slid his mouth away from hers again.

"Aha!" he whispered triumphantly, looking deep into her eyes and lifting a hand to caress the soft skin of her neck. "I knew it."

"Smarty-pants!" Kati teased, sliding a hand to the back of his head and pulling him close to try to claim his mouth again. Avoiding her searching mouth, Luke dipped his head to her neck, nibbling his way gently up to the lobe of her ear. Her heart thundered loudly in her breast, and his lips teased her.

"And there's more than business between us, isn't there, Kati Rose?" he whispered, his words soft and moist against her. Struggling to find her voice, her head fell back in wild abandon.

"Yes," she murmured, gasping as he tightened his arms around her waist and pulled her close until she was pressed against him. Luke's breathing was as fast as hers. His chest moved rhythmically against her breasts.

"I love you, Kati Rose," he whispered softly, finding her lips again to drop quick, hot kisses on her waiting, upturned mouth. His lips slid from her mouth to tease the soft satin of her neck. Luke loved her! Happiness shimmied down and through her, bringing a sweet joy to her heart.

"I—I—" She swallowed hard as his mouth moved over hers again. This time his lips were gently coaxing hers into submission. Hungrily, she kissed him back as desire roared through her, weakening her resistance.

"Kati?" Luke's husky whisper was soft against her cheek. He drew back to look at her. His face was so expectant, so hopeful, Kati lifted a hand to stroke his cheek. His skin was roughened from the stubble of his beard, prickly against her soft palm. Her eyes met his and Kati was certain she had never felt such pure, honest joy. It was overwhelming.

"I love you, too," Kati shouted, throwing her arms around Luke's neck, and nearly strangling him in her desire to hold him tight. "I love you! I love you!"

Hugging her in return, Luke laughed softly, the sound wonderful in the darkness. Sliding his hands through the curly strands of her hair, Luke tipped her head back and looked at her. His eyes slowly went over every familiar feature of her face and a soft smile tipped his lips. Had she been looking before, she would have noticed the love shining in his eyes before this. Still smiling, Luke gently lowered his mouth to hers and slowly, tenderly sipped at her mouth. Kati sighed. She was in love with Luke, and she couldn't remember ever feeling quite so wonderful.

Pulling his mouth from hers, Luke pressed her head into his shoulder and just stood there, holding her tight. Closing her eyes, Kati struggled to get her breathing back on a more even keel. The wonderful scent of Luke clung to his suit coat, and she savored the scent, inhaling deeply. She was certain that nothing had ever smelled so wonderful before. She rubbed her cheek against the rough material of his suit. She loved everything about him, his scent, his looks, his kisses. She loved him.

"Here you two are, I've been looking all over for you." Bessie peeked around the door. Kati tried to back out of Luke's arms, but he wouldn't let her. He kept his arm around her and held her tight.

"Hi, Bessie," he said quietly. "Need something?"

"Mr. Billings and Vera are at it again." Bessie shook her head. "Lunatics, I tell you. Vera needs to be relieved from the refreshment table before she dumps the punch over Mr. Billings's head. I told her I'd try to find you, Luke. Said you were supposed to be dancing. Kind of hard to dance out here with no music, isn't it?" she inquired, her eyes twinkling wickedly.

Kati lifted her head from Luke's shoulder and smiled at Bessie. "Depends on what kind of dancing you're talking about," she replied sassily, and Bessie's mouth fell open. Kati's smile grew. It was the first time she had ever seen Bessie speechless.

Luke turned to Kati, saw the look on her face and burst out laughing. "Come on, Kati Rose. I'd better take you inside." One dark brow rose wickedly. "I think you've had enough . . . *dancing* for one night." Putting an arm around each of them, Luke guided Bessie and Kati back inside.

"What happened?" Bessie hissed, hustling Kati into a corner behind the refreshment table after Luke had gone off to try to referee Vera and Mr. Billings.

"Happened?" Kati asked innocently. "Why, Bessie, what makes you think anything happened?" she teased, her eyes dancing in delight.

"Listen, Kati Rose," Bessie scolded, obviously not pleased with the answers she was getting. "I didn't come down with the last rain drop, you know. I been around some in my time—"

"You have?" Kati's eyes widened. "Tell me about it?" she asked, teasing Bessie unmercifully.

Bessie's eyes narrowed and her gaze swept Kati from head to toe. "You look different," she decided, sliding her gaze back up to Kati's. She looked at her for a long moment and her face broke into a happy smile. "I know what it is," Bessie whispered hurriedly. "You're in love, aren't you?" She laughed softly, not waiting for Kati to answer. "I knew it," Bessie cried, slapping a hand to her thigh. "I knew there was something special about that boy."

Bessie sighed heavily, shaking her head. "Kati Rose, it's high time you found yourself someone. And Lucas Kane is a pretty special someone."

Kati smiled, her eyes finding Luke over Bessie's head. "I know," she said dreamily.

Wilfred had strolled up to the table and was eyeing Bessie. Kati recognized the look in his eyes. It was the

same look Luke had when he looked at her. She smiled.
Wilfred was in love with Bessie. How wonderful. Kati
glanced back at Bessie, and couldn't help but wonder if
she knew.

"Uh, Bessie," Kati nodded toward the waiting man,
"Wilfred's waiting for you." Her words propelled Bessie around. She took one look at Wilfred and an engaging smile lit her face. Kati looked from one to the other.
They didn't know, she realized, watching them. They
didn't know they loved each other. Kati smiled. They
were going to be very interesting to watch.

"Would you like to dance, Bessie?" Wilfred asked
politely, and Bessie preened.

"Love to, Wilfred." She linked her arm through his.
Although she stood a good four inches taller than the
man, it didn't seem to bother her. They looked good together, Kati decided. Very good.

"The dance floor is so crowded, Bessie, Luke suggested we take our dance outdoors—where it's not quite
so crowded," he added quickly.

"Why, Wilfred," Bessie replied sweetly, hanging on to
his arm. "I'd love to." She turned and winked at Kati. "I
told you I liked that boy," she whispered for Kati's ears
only.

Love must be in the air and in her heart, Kati thought
dreamily as she began straightening the table. She looked
up and caught Luke watching her from across the room.
"I love you," she mouthed silently, and Luke smiled.

"I love you, too," he said loudly, causing every head
in the general vicinity to turn and look at him. A soft
ripple of laughter filled the room. Blushing, Kati re-

sisted the urge to duck her head and hide. She loved
Luke, and she didn't care who knew it. And apparently
neither did he.

Chapter Nine

Pacing in irritation, Kati pushed open the kitchen door and scanned the diner. "Luke, is she here yet?" she asked with a worried frown. Sensing her distress, Luke sighed heavily. Tossing down the paper he was reading, Luke rounded the counter, slid an arm around her waist and walked her back into the kitchen.

"Kati, will you please stop worrying? Bessie is a big girl. I'm sure she's fine. Besides, she's not that late." He glanced at the large clock hanging over the back door. "It's only ten, Kati. I'm sure she'll be here soon. Now stop worrying."

"But Luke," Kati said, still frowning. "No one has seen her since the dance Saturday night. You know very well almost everyone in town was at the lake yesterday, everyone except Bessie. *And* she's never been late before." Kati continued, certain she was building a viable case for the dastardly deed that had no doubt befallen Bessie. "Maybe I should take a run over to her house, just to check it out." Kati reached around to tug her apron off, but Luke stopped her midway and slid her apron back around her waist.

"You'll do no such thing," he instructed, his voice soft and indulgent as he dropped his hands to her shoulders to hold her in place. "I'm sure Bessie's fine. She'll probably come sashaying in here any minute. Now stop worrying," he scolded, dropping a quick kiss to her lips. "Now, you've got stew to make, and I've got to go do the set-ups before the lunch crowd arrives. Now try not to worry, please? She'll be here."

Trying to drag a smile to her trembling lips, Kati *tried* not to worry. But it was hard. It was so unlike Bessie to be late for work.

The last time she had seen Bessie was when Wilfred had escorted her from the refreshment stand Saturday night at the dance. When the dance ended, Luke had helped her clean up and transport the leftover food back to the diner. Bessie usually helped, but she was nowhere to be found.

As was customary on the day after the dance, most of the town assembled at the lake for a picnic. Kati and Luke had spent the day swimming, soaking up the sun, and just enjoying each other's company. Kati had not been too alarmed when Bessie hadn't appeared at the picnic. Bessie wasn't too fond of the hot June temperatures. But this morning, Bessie still hadn't shown up for work and Kati was nearly frantic. Pacing the kitchen in agitation, Kati jammed her hands into the pockets of her apron, her thoughts running rampant. Perhaps she should call the police? No, what on earth would I tell them? I've misplaced my waitress, could you find her for me? No, that would never do. Kati's face brightened. Maybe she should call Wilfred. He was the last person to see Bessie, maybe he'd know where she was. Crossing quickly to the phone, Kati dialed Wilfred's number, pacing back and forth and waiting for him to answer.

"You're going to pace a hole in the floor," Bessie announced, stepping calmly into the kitchen. Kati slammed down the phone and whirled on her.

"Where on earth have you been?" Kati demanded, her words coming out in a furious rush that caused Bessie's gray brows to rise in surprise.

"Why?" Bessie asked nonchalantly, bending to slip off her street shoes and slip on her white work shoes.

"Why?" Kati echoed, her tone dark. "Why? Because I've been worried sick about you. No one has seen you since the dance Saturday night. And you've never ever been late for work before," she added lamely, watching as Bessie gave her a strange look.

"Want to dock my pay?" Bessie asked flippantly, enjoying the stunned look on Kati's face.

"It has nothing to do with your pay. It has to do with caring. You scared the life out of me, Bessie."

Bessie smiled and reached out to pat Kati's arm. "Sorry, never thought to call and let you know I was all right. Guess I just got too involved."

"Involved? In what?" Kati looked at Bessie skeptically. She didn't look any the worse for the wear. "What was so all-fired important that you forgot to call?" she asked suspiciously.

"Well, if you must know, *Miss Nosy*," Bessie snapped defensively, placing her hands on her hips and daring Kati to say anything, "I've been with Wilfred."

"With Wilfred!" Kati's scowl deepened. "What on earth have you and Wilfred been doing for two days?"

"Things," Bessie retorted evasively, a secretive smile on her lips.

"What kind of things?" Kati persisted, wanting to make sure there was a good reason that she had been put through hell this morning.

"Things!" Bessie repeated emphatically, wiggling her brows suggestively. Kati's mouth fell open. She suddenly realized just what *things* Bessie and Wilfred had been doing.

"You and Wilfred?" Kati asked weakly, wondering if she appeared as dumb as she suddenly felt. She could feel the heat creep upward from her neck to her cheeks.

"Don't go looking so shocked," Bessie sniffed indignantly. "May not look like it, but there's still some embers left in this old stove." She chuckled softly, her face going dreamy. "Wilfred's too, if the truth be known," she whispered, glancing around to make certain no one but Kati could hear.

Laughing, Kati threw her arms around Bessie and gave her a hug. "I'm so happy for you both, Bessie." She planted a loud kiss on Bessie's cheek. "I think it's wonderful. But the least you could have done was call me so I wouldn't worry," she scolded good-naturedly.

"Kati Rose, do I look like I need a keeper? Now how about telling me what's going on with you and Luke?" Just the sound of his name caused Kati to beam.

"After the dance Saturday, he walked me home. And yesterday we went to the lake together. That's about it." That wasn't quite the truth, but it was good enough for now.

"That's it?" Bessie frowned, her full mouth pulling down in the effort.

Kati tried not to grin. That wasn't *quite* it, but that was all she was willing to divulge. What she had with Luke was so new, so special, she wanted to keep it inside for now, savoring the wonderful feel of it. She loved him so.

"Kati." Bessie looked at her and Kati could have sworn there was a tear in her gruff gray eyes. "I've known you your whole life. Knew your mama and your papa, too. I had almost given up hope of you ever finding someone. You're so stubborn and prideful, and much too independent for your own good. Luke is a good man. I knew that the first time I laid eyes on him."

"I know, Bessie." Kati couldn't help but wonder what Bessie was driving at. She didn't have to sell Kati on Luke, she was in love with the man.

"Just remember, your independence and this diner aren't going to keep you warm at night. You need a man, Kati, and Lucas Kane is that man. Don't go letting nothing come between you. What you've got is special. For the first time in your whole life, Kati, I can see you're happy. You've done for Patrick and everyone else. Now it's time to do for you." Bessie leaned over and kissed Kati's cheek. "Now hand me that apron over there and let me get to work. Oh, Wilfred's out front, and the man's starving. He wants a sandwich and some of those new chips of ours."

Going to the pantry, Kati grabbed one of the boxes down and pulled loose several bags of chips and tossed them at Bessie. There was a soft knock at the back door.

"You go on out front and take care of Wilfred," Kati instructed. "I'll get the door." Kati pulled open the door. Her eyes widened and a delighted whoop fell from her lips.

"Hi, Sis!"

"Patrick!" Kati squealed, throwing her arms around him and pulling him inside. "Oh, Patrick." She pulled back to get a good look at him. "You look wonderful." Tears of happiness filled her eyes. It had been so long since she'd seen him, she could hardly believe he was here. Luke was here, Patrick was home and everything was wonderful. "Let me look at you." She walked a circle around him, frowning gently. "You're too skinny," she finally announced, stopping in front of him to plant a kiss on his cheek. "And you need a haircut," she scolded gently, causing Patrick to chuckle softly.

"And you haven't changed a bit." Although younger than Kati, Patrick stood a good ten inches above her. His hair was a brighter shade of auburn, but his eyes were the same emerald green as her own.

"How long are you staying?" Kati asked.

"Just a little while." Patrick shifted nervously. "I just wanted to stop by to see how you were getting on."

"I'm getting on fine. Wait till Bessie sees you," Kati exclaimed in delight. As much as Bessie proclaimed that Patrick needed a good switching, Bessie, like nearly everyone else, loved Patrick. Despite his immaturity, Patrick was a sweet, gentle man who had inherited all of the charm of his Irish ancestors.

"I can see not much has changed around here," Patrick commented, glancing around. He inhaled deeply. "This is Monday, so I'll bet you're making the famous Ryan Stew."

"Are you hungry?" Kati asked worriedly, and Patrick laughed again.

"Still playing mother hen?" Patrick teased, ruffling her hair. "Kati, I'm a big boy. You don't have to worry about me anymore."

Kati frowned. She wasn't so sure about that. She couldn't help but wonder what had brought Patrick home. She hoped he wasn't in trouble again.

"How is business?" Patrick asked, picking a carrot up off the counter and popping it into his mouth. "Are you and Bessie handling things all right?"

Kati laughed softly. "It's not just Bessie and me anymore, Luke's here. He's been here for over a month, and I can't— Patrick, what's wrong?"

His face had gone white. "Lucas Kane is . . . here?"

Kati frowned. "Well, of course, I thought you knew—"

"What's he doing here?" Patrick hissed, looking quickly at the door as if he expected the devil himself to walk through any minute.

"Patrick," Kati grabbed his arm, as her suspicions grew. "What do you mean what's he doing here? Didn't you know—"

"Kati, Mr. Billings wants to know if you've got a fresh bone—" Luke stopped dead in his tracks when he saw Patrick, and Patrick seemed to shrink away from him. Kati looked from one man to the other wondering what was going on.

"What on earth is wrong with you two?" she demanded suspiciously.

"Hello, Patrick," Luke said softly, but there was a thread of steel in his voice.

"Luke." Patrick shifted nervously from one foot to the other. "What are you doing here?" Kati's confusion grew as she watched the two men.

Luke let the kitchen door swing shut slowly behind him as he walked into the room and faced Patrick. "I think you know what I'm doing here," Luke said quietly, and Kati had a sudden urge to jump between the men. She didn't like the sound of things, and a deep-seated fear slowly bubbled inside of her.

Patrick let loose a deep sigh. "Don't worry, Luke. I've got your money."

"Money?" Kati looked at her brother. "What are you talking about, Patrick? What money?"

"Kati," Luke said softly, trying to corral her next to him. It was important that he get a chance to explain things to her in the proper way. He didn't want her jumping to conclusions. Kati looked at him closely, refusing to budge. "This is between your brother and me," Luke added as Kati turned to him, her body suddenly trembling in fear.

"If it concerns my brother and *my* diner," she added, feeling torn between the two, "then it concerns me, too."

"Kati, now don't get upset," Patrick cautioned. "Luke lent me some money."

"And," she prompted, knowing her brother's penchant for running at the first sign of trouble. She had a feeling there was a lot more to this story than met the eye.

"And I guess I—" Patrick jammed a hand through his hair, and sighed again. "And I guess I disappeared without paying him back."

"You owe Luke money?" she asked weakly, feeling the floor beneath her begin to slowly sway.

"I gave him my half of the diner as collateral. I was going to pay him back, Kati, honest. It just, well, things didn't work out as I planned." Patrick looked at her, his face wreathed in sorrow. "I never figured he'd come here looking for me."

Patrick's words caused her legs to buckle, and Kati grabbed on to the counter to keep from falling. Oh God, she could feel her heart shattering into a million little pieces. It was all suddenly very clear why Luke was here, why he had insisted on staying. Tears burned her eyes, but she blinked them away. Now she finally understood Luke's reasons. He didn't care about her, or the diner. All he cared about was getting his money back from Patrick. Numbness overtook her as a cold, frigid chill penetrated her spirit. Patrick's other friends had taken her money and her hospitality, but Lucas Kane had taken her heart. And her love. Oh God, what a fool she had been! What a blind, trusting fool!

"Patrick," she said quietly, trying to stop the intense pounding in her head, and hoping her voice didn't betray her emotions. "Go on upstairs and rest. I'll handle this," she whispered, turning her stricken eyes to her brother. Patrick hesitated for just a moment and then turned and fled out the door.

"Don't you think it's about time you stop handling everything for your brother?" Luke gently touched her shoulder. "He's a big boy, Kati. Maybe it's time you let him take care of himself." His words caused the hurt to bubble to the surface. How dare he say such a thing to her! Taking a deep, controlling breath, Kati whirled on him. The look in his eyes caused the hurt to deepen. She had trusted him, needed him. And he had devastated her.

"Get out," she ordered, her words coming out on a shaky breath. "Get out of my diner, and out of my life. Now!" Her eyes blazed in hurt and desolation.

"Kati, listen to me, let me explain," Luke pleaded, taking her hands in his. "It's not what you think."

She yanked her hands free. "You lied to me. You don't care about me," she cried, praying she could control the flood of tears that threatened to fall. "And you don't care about my diner. All you care about is your precious money. You knew sooner or later Patrick would come back. That's why you came here, and that's why you stayed, isn't it?" she demanded, daring him to deny it. "Isn't it!"

"Kati, you're not being rational. If you'll just give me a chance to—"

"Rational!" she blazed. The man had used her, betrayed her and broken her heart and now he wanted her to be rational? "Get out!" she shrieked, pushing him away. "I don't want you here, and I don't want you in my life."

"Kati, you don't mean that. I love you. I need you." There was a soft plea in his words, but she heard none of it.

Love? The word seemed to shrivel up and die in her mind. She had been such a fool. She had loved him. Needed him. And now...

"The only thing you needed me for was to get your money back," she whispered, her voice breaking on the words. "Don't worry, Luke, I'll make sure you get your money. Now please, get out." The pressure around her heart tightened, and she turned her back to him, not wanting him to see her anguish. She heard the kitchen door swing shut, and she expelled a deep, choking breath.

What a fool she had been. What a blind, trusting fool. "Oh God," she whimpered. The tears came, sliding unheeded down her cheeks. Great wracking sobs shook her body, and she leaned against the counter, knowing she couldn't support her weight anymore. "Oh Luke," she whimpered, feeling the pain seep into every inch of her. She loved him, and he had used her. And Kati knew she would never be able to forgive him.

"Kati Rose, what the devil is going on?" Bessie skidded into the kitchen and came to an abrupt halt when she spotted Kati. "Kati, what is it, honey? What's wrong?" Bessie touched her shoulder, and Kati turned into her waiting arms.

"Oh, Bessie," she sobbed. "Luke lied to me, he used me. He doesn't care about me, or the diner." She stopped to wipe at her tears. "The only reason he came here is because Patrick owed him money. He's been hanging around waiting for Patrick to show up." Her words and her breath came out in short, gaspy jerks.

"Now who told you those lies?" Bessie demanded, touching Kati's cheek. "I'm sure it's all a misunderstanding, Kati Rose. Don't worry, I'm sure you and Luke will patch things up. He loves you, honey," Bessie said gently, and Kati shook her head. Wiping away her tears, Kati pulled herself upright.

"Love?" She laughed bitterly. "The only thing Luke cares about is his money. And no, Bessie, it's not a misunderstanding. I understand perfectly." Grabbing a tissue, Kati mopped her face and blew her nose. Her heart may be broken, but at least she still had her diner. The thought did nothing to cheer her. What good would her precious diner be without Luke and his love? Another wave of tears threatened to spill down her cheeks.

"Now, Kati," Bessie soothed. "Just give him a chance to explain. I'm sure once you hear him out—"

"There's nothing to explain, Bessie," Kati said wearily, shaking her head, and trying to shake off the pain. But it wouldn't go away. "I just threw Luke out of here, and if he shows his face in here again I want you to..." Kati closed her eyes and pressed her hands over them, hoping to stop the flood of tears. Taking a deep breath, she lifted her chin. "If that man shows his face in here, I want you to shoot him!"

"Here we go again," Bessie sighed, shaking her head.

"Can you handle things here for awhile?" Kati asked, yanking off her apron and smoothing back the damp hair from her face. "I need to go upstairs and talk to Patrick."

Bessie grumbled. "Should have figured that boy was back. That explains what all the trouble's about. Kati

Rose, I told you, that boy needed a good switching years ago...."

"Not now, Bessie," Kati pleaded, touching her throbbing head. She couldn't deal with any more problems at the moment. "I'll be back in a little bit." Kati slipped out the back door of the diner and up the stairs to her apartment.

"Patrick? Where are you?" She stalked through the rooms until she found him lying across the bed in his old room. "Patrick!"

"Kati, I'm sorry. I had no idea he would show up here. Did Luke cause you any trouble? Did he hurt you?" She lifted a hand and touched his face. Poor, sweet, irresponsible Patrick.

Kati shook her head, and tried not to cry again. What Luke did to her had nothing to do with Patrick. And she didn't want to admit what a fool she'd been. It wasn't Patrick's fault that she'd fallen in love with him. It was her own. But, the knowledge only made her heart ache more.

"Do you have the money you owe Luke?" she asked, sitting down wearily on one corner of the bed.

"It's right here in my shirt." Patrick pulled loose a wad of bills and gave them to Kati. She didn't even bother to count them. She didn't want to know just how much her love had cost her. "What are you going to do, Kati?"

"I'm going to buy my diner back," she declared firmly, shoving the money in the back pocket of her jeans. "Now get some rest. I'll be back up after the diner closes. I'll send Bessie up with some food for you."

"Kati?" Patrick looked like a lost little boy again, and her heart went out to him.

"What?" she asked softly.

"I'm sorry, Sis."

Kati bent down and kissed his cheek. "Don't worry about it, Patrick. I'll take care of it." Her shoulders slumped in defeat. Didn't she always? Didn't she always take care of everything, handle everything, until Luke came along?

She made it to Vera's house in three minutes flat, running all the way. Taking a deep breath, she pounded on the door. She knew Luke was here, and alone, because Vera was still at the diner.

His face brightened when he saw her. "Kati!" Luke slid his arms around her waist and pulled her close before she knew what he was doing. For just an instant, Kati closed her eyes and allowed herself the luxury of being in his arms. Tears threatened to spill over when she realized it would be the last time. She loved him, but he had used and betrayed her. And she knew she would never, ever, trust or allow anyone to do it to her again.

"Luke?" She pushed out of his arms and pulled the money from her jeans. "Here's the money Patrick owes you. Now I believe you have something of his?"

Luke looked down at the money and back up at her. "Kati, this isn't necessary. If you'd just let me explain."

"There's nothing to explain. You've got your money. Now I want the papers Patrick signed back. You remember those, don't you?" she asked bitterly, her voice thin and high. "The papers you flashed under my nose the day you arrived. You've got your money, I want the papers and my diner back."

Luke looked at her for a long time. And for an instant, she feared she might soften. She loved him so, all she wanted to do was wake up and find out that this was all a misunderstanding. But it wasn't, it was reality.

Finally, sighing deeply, Luke pulled the papers out of his back pocket and handed them to her.

"Thank you," she said coldly, squeezing the papers tightly in her fist.

"This isn't the end of it, Kati Rose Ryan," Luke threatened as she turned down the walk. "It's not going to be that easy to get rid of me. I love you."

Kati stopped and turned back to look at him. "Lucas Kane, if you show your face in my diner again, I'll have you arrested for trespassing."

His soft laughter followed her as she turned and ran toward the diner, and it only made her furious.

"After I shoot you!" she yelled over her shoulder.

Chapter Ten

"Kati Rose, it's been two days. How much longer are you going to keep up this nonsense?" Bessie demanded, looking at Kati shrewdly.

Kati shrugged her shoulders. She and Bessie had been going around and around about Luke ever since Kati had thrown him out of the diner. She could not get Bessie to understand or admit that whatever she and Luke had was over.

"It's not nonsense," Kati insisted, not bothering to look up from the cupcakes she was half-heartedly mixing. Even now, just talking about Luke, thinking about him, brought a shaft of pain to her heart. "I told you, Bessie. It's over. Lucas Kane is out of my life *and*," she added pointedly, looking up at Bessie, "out of *my* diner. It's for the best," Kati said softly, wishing she could convince herself of that. For two days she hadn't eaten, and she hadn't slept. Thoughts of Luke tormented her.

Would she ever be able to walk in here and not think of him, not see his dark head, not hear his laughter, not smell the masculine scent of him? She had tried to carry on as usual, but it was hard. She put on the calmest face she could while at the diner. It was only when she was safely alone upstairs that the tears came. Kati knew that, no matter how she tried, she would never be able to forget about Luke. No matter what, she still loved him, and, she realized, she did need him. But, it was a little too late to think about that. She had taught herself not to need anyone once before. Surely she could do it again, couldn't she?

"You need that boy, Kati," Bessie scolded. "And it's about time you realize it, before it's too late."

"I don't need anybody," Kati lied, whipping the cupcakes viciously with a wooden spoon. "I did fine before, and I'll do fine now. Besides, I've got you." Kati glanced up and tried to smile, but it died somewhere between her heart and her mouth.

Watching her, Bessie muttered something under her breath.

"Bessie." Kati sighed, she wasn't up to talking about this anymore. How on earth was she going to forget about Luke if all Bessie and everyone else in town did was constantly remind her? She knew no matter what, she'd never forget Luke. He was a part of her—a sad and lonely part, now.

"All right, all right." Bessie grabbed a tray of clean dishes and headed for the door. "Patrick's out front, says he wants to talk to you. And Vera and Mr. Billings are fighting again. They've squared off right smack dab in the middle of the diner, and I can't get a lick of work done with them two yapping."

Kati sighed. She didn't need any more problems. She could barely deal with the ones she had. Just breathing was a chore, now. Everything was a chore without Luke.

"What are they arguing about now?" Kati asked.

"Who's going to sit in what booth."

"But Bessie, I thought Luke handled—" She caught herself. Luke was gone and *she* was the only one left to take care of things now.

"What are we going to do?" Bessie inquired, cocking her head.

Kati sighed. "What we've always done. Handle things. Go tell Patrick I'll be with him in a moment. I'll take care of Vera and Mr. Billings first."

"Lunatics," Bessie mumbled, pushing through the door with Kati on her heels.

Ignoring Patrick for the moment, she crossed over to where Vera and Mr. Billings were standing toe to toe, yelling at each other.

"Vera, Mr. Billings, what's the matter?" She looked from one to the other. They were glaring at each other, and Mr. Billings had Beauregard cradled in his arms. It was all Kati needed now. If Tibbits showed up and closed her down because of that blasted dog! Luke had saved her once...Luke. Everything she was, everything she wanted was Luke. But Luke was gone now, she realized sadly, and she had no one to depend on but herself.

"Mr. Billings, what on earth is Beauregard doing in here? You know I told you he couldn't come in here anymore." Going straight past tact, Kati went straight for the truth. Bessie was right, these two were lunatics. "You're going to get me closed down," she threatened.

Vera's chin lifted, and she smiled smugly. "I told you, Mr. Billings," Vera caroled in a singsong voice before turning to Kati. "I told him you wouldn't allow that mutt in here, but would he listen to me? No." She turned back to glare at Mr. Billings. "*He* thinks he's so smart, he won't listen to anybody!"

"I am smart!" Mr. Billings retorted, glaring at her over the top of his glasses. "Smart enough to know that *you're sitting in my booth*." He glanced down at Beauregard. "Our booth," he corrected, giving the old hound dog an affectionate pat on the head.

"Any man who talks to a dog can't be very smart," Vera retorted. "And it's not your booth, *it's mine*. Luke gave it to me. Because *I'm* the number one customer here."

"You are not!" Mr. Billings yelled, startling poor Beauregard who began to whine.

"Am so!" Vera declared, nudging closer and causing her flowered hat to slip down and sit crookedly on her forehead. "Luke said so!"

"This dog has more brains than you'll ever have, Vera Wilson. At least *he* cares about me!"

Kati's startled gaze flew to Mr. Billings. Why did she get the feeling these two were not arguing about the dog, the booth, or who the number one customer was, but something altogether different?

"I care about you, too," Vera snapped, giving her hat a hearty shove.

"Then why'd you say you wouldn't marry me?" Mr. Billings demanded, glaring at Vera, and daring her to answer. Kati was really confused, looking from one to the other. What on earth was going on? Mr. Billings asked Vera to marry him? She bit back a smile. Good Lord, they'd kill each other before the honeymoon was over.

"Because *you* don't even know how to propose decently," Vera whined in a hurt voice.

"What's wrong with the way I proposed?" Mr. Billings demanded, pushing his face into Vera's again.

Taking a deep, shuddering breath, Vera tried to control herself. *"Mr. Billings,"* she declared haughtily, lifting her chin and drawing the words out carefully, "no woman wants to be told it will be cheaper living together than living apart. That's no kind of proposal."

"Well, it's the truth, ain't it?" Mr. Billings countered, and Kati's eyes flew back to him. This was getting interesting, she decided. "It *will* be cheaper for us to live together, than to live apart. So what's wrong with that?"

"No woman wants to be treated like...like...a tax deduction!" Vera shuddered. "That's not the way to propose. Any *fool* knows that!"

"Who you calling a fool, Vera Wilson?" Mr. Billings yelled, and Kati quickly jumped between them. This wasn't getting interesting, it was getting dangerous.

"That's enough!" Kati yelled and they both turned to stare at her. "Now, both of you stop this right now!" she instructed, her voice stern.

"Kati Rose! What on earth's the matter with you?" Vera asked, clearly confused. "Why are you yelling at us?" Vera glanced at Mr. Billings and Kati could see they were about to join forces and leave her hanging out here in the middle—again. She should have known better than to try coming between these two.

"Where's Luke?" Vera asked suddenly, glancing around. "*He'd* know how to settle this. He knows how to settle everything. And *he* never yelled at us," she scolded, looking at Kati as if she'd taken leave of her senses.

"Yes, where is Lucas?" Mr. Billings asked, jumping on the bandwagon. "He'll be able to settle this. He can handle anything, can't he, Vera?" They both turned to look at her, and Kati sighed and shook her head. At the moment these two weren't the only ones who needed Luke, she thought sadly. But Luke wasn't here anymore, and she didn't want to go into a lengthy explanation as to why, particularly to Vera. She knew how attached Vera was to Luke. There was no sense upsetting her anymore than she already was. She'd have to remedy this on her own. But Kati had to admit, she wished Luke was here too.

"Vera, do you want to marry Mr. Billings?" Kati asked, no longer willing to put up with any more nonsense from these two.

Vera fluffed her hair. "Well, I'd like to. If the man would propose properly," she added, glaring at Mr. Billings. He opened his mouth to say something, but quickly Kati raised her hand to stop him.

"And you, Mr. Billings," she asked. "Do you want to marry Vera?"

"I asked her, didn't I?" he grumbled, glancing up at Vera.

Thinking quickly, Kati grabbed each of their arms and walked them toward the door. "It's only three o'clock. If you hurry, you can get to the Village Hall and get your license before they close." They both opened their mouths to protest, but Kati pushed them out of the diner and slammed the door behind them. "Hurry up, now," she called through the glass. "You don't want to be late." Heaving a sigh of relief, Kati slumped against the door.

"That was some mighty fancy footwork, Kati Rose," Bessie called from behind the counter. "One down, one to go." She nodded toward Patrick who was sitting at a back booth drinking coffee.

Kati nodded and headed toward her brother. She hoped that Patrick had his fill of roaming around the country. She hoped that now he was ready to settle down, stay in Libertyville and work the diner. With Luke gone, she really could use another helping hand, she decided, wondering how on earth she had managed before Luke arrived.

"Patrick, you wanted to see me?"

"Kati Rose." Patrick blushed and Kati got the feeling this was going to be another one of Patrick's schemes. She decided she had better sit down.

"I, well—I'm—going to head over to Kansas City..."

"You're leaving?" Kati's face fell. "But Patrick, you just got here. And what are you going to use for money? You know very well I don't have any!" Kati clenched her teeth, trying not to show how furious she was with her brother. He had sailed back into her life, totally disrupted it, and now he announced he was leaving, without even caring whether she might need his help or not. Luke had been right, she thought sadly. Maybe it was time that she started letting Patrick handle things on his own. If he wanted to leave, broke or not, she'd let him. It was time she made it clear to him, she was no longer going to bail him out of trouble. He was going to have to stand on his own two feet. It was time for Patrick to grow up.

"Kati, don't worry, I don't need any money."

Kati rubbed her head. It wasn't her problem anymore, she decided, forcing herself not to interfere. If Patrick was going to learn to stand on his own two feet, there was no better time than the present. She wasn't going to ask where he had gotten the money. As long as it wasn't from her, she wasn't going to worry.

"All right, Patrick. But this time, you're on your own. You're my brother and I love you, but I'm not going to bail you out of any more jams. Understand?" Patrick blushed and then nodded. At least he knew the score, she thought tiredly.

"I'd better get going." Patrick stood up and kissed her cheek. "Bye, Sis," Patrick said softly, then walked out the door.

Kati stood staring after him. Patrick was gone again and she was left all alone. Bessie had Wilfred. Mr. Billings had Vera. And what did she have? She had her independence and her diner, and Kati knew it would never be enough.

"Oh, Luke," she murmured, glancing around the empty diner as tears filled her eyes.

"Kati Rose! You'd better come quick, all hell's broke loose!" Bessie's voice rose in panic as she skidded into the kitchen.

Kati glanced at her. She had dealt with her brother and Vera, Mr. Billings, and even old Beauregard today and Kati wasn't sure she could handle anything else. Or even wanted to.

"Now what?" she asked without looking up, trying to concentrate on the pudding she was attempting to make. As far as she was concerned, all hell could break loose, so long as it didn't bother her or require her attention. Right now, it was an effort just to handle herself.

"There's a construction crew out front. They're blocking all our parking spaces and barricading our street."

"And?" Kati prompted, knowing she hadn't heard the worst of it.

"And there's a man out front says he's got to talk to you right away!"

"Damnation!" Kati muttered, grabbing a towel to wipe her hands. "Bessie, calm down. I'll handle it," she said with more confidence than she felt, even though she didn't want to deal with anything right now. All Kati really wanted to do was curl up in her bed and have a good cry.

"You'd better hurry up," Bessie encouraged, grabbing Kati's arm and dragging her toward the door. "Come on, now. I don't like the looks of this."

"Bessie!" Kati protested, allowing herself to be pulled along, despite her tiredness. Squaring her shoulders, she took a deep breath and swung through the door. Kati came to an abrupt halt. Her gaze skipped across the patterned linoleum floor, up past the worn work boots, which were planted firmly in the middle of her diner. Her eyes skipped up the long legs encased by worn jeans faded nearly white in places, up and across the blue work shirt stretched across shoulders that seemed a mile wide. The sleeves of his shirt were rolled up to reveal bronzed muscular forearms. And a tattoo.

Luke. Her breathing slowed, and then kicked in again. Her back went up immediately.

"What are you doing here?" she demanded. Oh Lord, he looked so good. Her eyes caressed him, loving him, missing him.

"I came to talk to you," he said softly, reaching out a hand to brush a curl from her cheek. Kati recoiled from his touch, torn between throwing herself at him, and tossing him out on his ear. If Luke touched her, she'd be a goner. Kati wasn't as strong as she thought she was. She knew it. But judging from the look on Luke's face, he knew it too.

"There's nothing to talk about," Kati said firmly, turning on her heel and attempting to storm away. Luke caught her around the waist, and the breath went out of her in a whoosh as he scooped her up off the floor and threw her over his shoulders like a sack of potatoes.

"Lucas Kane!" Kati roared when she got her breath back. "Put me down!" She pounded on his back, but he paid her no mind. Ignoring her, Luke marched toward the door.

"Put me down!" she screeched again, pounding on his hard hat now in order to get his attention and let him know she meant business. "Bessie! Call the police!"

"Sorry," Bessie called back, smiling broadly. "I don't seem to recall the number. Besides, Kati Rose, you know I never stick my nose where it doesn't belong."

"Bessie," Luke called over his shoulder. "Mind the diner until we get back!"

"Sure thing," she called and Kati lifted her head to glare at her.

"Traitor!" Kati yelled, furious at the soft chuckle that shook the woman's frame.

Luke kicked open the door with his booted foot and marched outside. "I'm going to put you down, Kati," he warned. "But only if you promise to hear me out. Okay?" She gave him another thump on his back, and he took that as her answer. Gently, Luke let her slide the length of him and set her on her feet on the sidewalk. Kati immediately turned to bolt, but Luke grabbed the back of her blouse and reined her in.

"Let go of me!" she hissed, twisting and trying to slap his hands away. "Haven't you done enough? Leave me alone." Tears threatened the back of her eyes, and she bitterly swallowed them back.

"I told you once before, Kati," Luke said, grinning. "I'm not going anywhere. *Ever.*"

"What the hell do you think you're doing?" she demanded, glaring up into his handsome face.

"Well, honey," he queried, smiling down at her and brushing the tangled hair out of her face. "What does it look like I'm doing?"

"Besides kidnapping me?" she countered, her voice loud and furious. Luke chuckled softly and hugged her close. She struggled to break loose from his arms. She couldn't very well think or do much else with him so close. Her breath caught. Giving herself a mental shake, Kati tried not to let the man affect her. But it was hard.

"Is this about right, boss?" one of the workmen called, and Luke turned to the sign above the diner, keeping his arm carefully around her.

"That's perfect, Ralph. Just perfect."

Kati glared at Luke. "What's perfect? What on earth are they— Luke! Stop them! They're taking down my sign." Fuming, Kati started toward the man. "Don't you touch my sign!" she yelled, fully intending to do bodily harm to the sign remover if she got her hands on him. Luke grabbed the back of her shirt again and held on tight.

"Kati Rose." He sighed and tried to hide the smile that was threatening to break loose. "If you'll just be patient—"

"I don't want to be patient," she cried, twisting around to slap at his hand which was clutching the back of her. Again. "I want to know why those men are taking down my sign. Who gave them permission?"

"I did," Luke returned smoothly, enjoying the fury that crossed her face.

"How dare you!" she hissed, giving him a good whack on the arm. "Haven't you done enough?"

"Kati Rose!" Vera hurried up the street. "What are you doing to Luke now? Why are you hitting him?" Vera was dragging Mr. Billings by the arm, and he in turn was dragging poor Beauregard by the leash as man and dog struggled to keep up with a hurrying Vera. Kati sighed. What was *she* doing to Luke? That was the pot calling the kettle black!

"Leave 'em alone, Vera!" Bessie called from the doorway. Puffing out her ample chest, Bessie looked fully prepared to throw herself bodily between Luke and Vera in an effort to let things be.

"I'm glad you're all here," Luke said, looking at the assembled group with a smile, and grabbing a tighter hold on Kati's shirt as she struggled to get away. Wilfred was peeking around Bessie, and vying for doorway space in order to see. Vera, Mr. Billings *and* Beauregard were standing there watching. And waiting. "You can all see our new sign," Luke continued.

"What do you mean *our* new sign?" Kati hissed. Standing on tiptoe, she glared into Luke's amused face, trying to ignore Vera and Mr. Billings who were now trying to hang on to her every word. "This is *my* diner, Lucas Kane," she yelled, poking his chest for emphasis after each word. "And *my* sign. You keep your darn hands off of it."

"It's not your sign Kati," Luke said softly. "It's *ours*. Look." He pointed to the new sign that was just being hoisted out and Kati's eyes widened as the new name registered.

Kane and Mabel's

The assembled crew broke into applause as the beautiful new sign was set in place, and Kati whirled on Luke, tears filling in her eyes. She opened her mouth to speak, trying to talk around the lump in her throat and then promptly snapped her mouth shut again, fearing she would only start blubbering. At one time, the new sign would have brought tears of joy and euphoria, now the sight of it only brought a decided sadness of what could have been. Tears spilled down her cheeks, and she was powerless to stop them.

"Lucas Kane, you leave my sign and my diner alone," she cried, her words trembling across her lips. How dare he touch her sign. Hadn't he done enough?

"It's not yours," Luke corrected. "It's ours."

"Patrick paid you back the money, and I have the papers for the diner," Kati snapped. "So how could the diner be *ours*?"

"You *had* the papers for the diner," he corrected, pulling a wrinkled wad from his jeans pocket. "Yesterday, Patrick and I made a deal. He sold me his half of the diner outright."

"What!" Kati grabbed the paper out of Luke's hand and read carefully. Her eyes rounded in stunned surprise as the anger flew out of her in a rush. "Luke, you can't be serious? You didn't really pay Patrick this much money for his share of the diner?" She could have bought a shopping center with what Luke had paid Patrick for the diner. And still have change left over.

Smiling, Luke nodded. "I would have paid any price, Kati, any price at all. I'd have given Patrick anything to have the diner."

"But Luke, you gave Patrick ten times what the diner is worth!"

"I know it," he said hurriedly. "But I told you, the money doesn't matter. What matters is you," Luke said tenderly, draping an arm around her.

"You had no right," she cried, slapping his arm away from her shoulder. How could she think clearly with him so close, with him touching her? The man's mere nearness scrambled her brains, and she needed to think now. To sort things out.

"Kati Rose, what on earth is wrong with you? You shouldn't be yelling at Luke like that. Why, my dear girl, you're going to hurt his feelings." Vera reached out and patted Luke's arm. He turned to flash Kati a wicked smile.

"I'm going to hurt a lot more than just his feelings," Kati muttered under her breath, glaring at the three of them. It wasn't enough that she had to deal with Luke, and a bunch of strange workmen. Now Vera had to get into the act, too. She glanced around, adding Bessie, Wilfred and even old Beauregard to the list.

"Come on, Kati." Tucking her under his arm, Luke guided her behind the pickup truck so they could have some privacy.

Swiping at her eyes, Kati gathered her dwindling fury. "Luke, how dare you—"

"Kati," Luke said tenderly, backing up against the truck and lifting a thumb to wipe her tears. "Shut up!"

"How dare you—I will not—" His lips came down on hers, fast and hard. For a moment she struggled, trying to push him away, but Luke caught her hands and trapped them to his chest, hauling her close so she couldn't move, couldn't speak, and couldn't wiggle away.

A low moan gurgled deep within her throat and without thinking, only feeling, Kati's arms went around him, her fingers sliding to tangle in the dark strands of his hair.

Luke's breathing was ragged as he slid his mouth from hers. "Now not a word until I'm finished, all right?" Wide-eyed, Kati stared at him. "All right?" he prompted, dropping another kiss to her unsuspecting mouth, and she finally nodded. She'd hear him out, listen to what he had to say, and then—then—she'd send him packing, with his new sign!

"I did loan Patrick the money, and when I first came to Libertyville it was to wait around for him. I knew sooner or later he'd show up and then I'd get my money back. When he put the diner up as collateral, I never dreamed I'd end up wanting the place, or working it. But, that was before I met you." He lifted his hands and gently cradled her tear-streaked face. "From the moment I met you, Kati, I knew I wanted you. You were so different, so special. For the first time in my life, I feel like I belong." He glanced around at the familiar town. "I belong here in Libertyville, with you. *We* belong together. I love you, Kati Rose."

Sniffling harder now, Kati clutched the front of his shirt and buried her face in it, her mind swirling. Luke loved her. Then why hadn't he been honest with her from the beginning? Oh Lord, she wanted to send him away. But she also wanted him to stay. She didn't know what she wanted. Except Luke.

"Why didn't you just tell me the truth, Luke?" she asked, not lifting her face, and trying not to sniffle. "Why?" Her voice was cracked and muffled.

"Kati Rose, if you remember correctly, I had my hands full just trying to get around all those barricades you kept throwing up in my face. You were so certain that I was a threat to you, your diner and your independence. I worked hard trying to prove that you didn't have to be afraid of me, that you could trust me." Sighing heavily, Luke ran a hand through his hair. "I guess I blew it," he said sadly. "I never meant to hurt you, Kati. All I want is another chance." She lifted her head and met his gaze. His eyes were filled with love and with regret.

"Oh Luke," she said, her breath catching in her throat.

"I love you, Kati, more than I've ever loved anyone." Instinctively, she raised a hand to caress his face, to erase the pain she saw reflected there. "I never meant to hurt you," he said again, and her heart went out to him. "Can you give me, give us, another chance?"

Lord, she loved him so much, she loved everything about him. Could she afford not to give him a chance? He was everything to her. Everything.

"Despite what you think, Kati, *you do need me*, as much as I need you. I was afraid if I told you the truth you'd throw me out on my ear. Which, if you remember, is exactly what you did." His eyes twinkled mischievously. "After you threatened to shoot me," he reminded her, and Kati chuckled softly, wiping away her tears.

"Kati?" Luke was looking at her with such love in his eyes, she felt her knees weaken. "Will you forgive me?" he whispered, and she hesitated only a moment, realizing finally how much she really did need him. Nothing was any good without him. She loved him and she needed him, and she was going to take her chances. Luke was everything to her. She nodded.

"And will you…" Luke stopped, his eyes caressing her face.

"What?" she whispered, feeling slightly breathless as he slid his arms around her and drew her closer. Luke's mouth found hers and desire tore through her. Kati arched close to him, feeling her body tense and tighten in response to him. She needed him and he needed her, and she knew no matter what, she had to take a chance. She had to. Oh Lord, she loved him so much. She clung to him, burying her head in the soft pad of his shoulder, and held on tight.

"Will you hurry up and ask her?" Bessie yelled, leading the parade coming around the side of the truck to watch the goings-on.

"It's getting hot out here!" Mr. Billings grumbled, mopping his brow.

"You're not going to yell at Luke anymore, are you?" Vera asked in concern, obviously not caring in the least that yelling wasn't what was on Kati's mind at the moment.

Kati and Luke looked at the assembled crowd, then at each other, and burst into laughter.

"This isn't exactly how I planned this," he whispered. "Kati Rose Ryan," Luke said softly, "will you marry me?"

"Say it louder," Wilfred called. "We all couldn't hear you."

"You weren't supposed to," Kati called back.

"Kati Rose, don't get huffy, now," Bessie called. "What's going on?" she asked, trying to inch closer and being very obvious. "Well?" she demanded, planting her hands on her hips.

Kati looked at Luke and burst out laughing. "Luke asked me to marry him." Kati smiled at Luke, her heart bursting with love.

"Well, what are you waiting for?" Bessie demanded. "Answer the man!"

Kati looked at all of them—Bessie and Wilfred, Vera and Mr. Billings, and even poor Beauregard, who flopped to the ground in boredom, yawning loudly and covering his eyes with his furry paws, clearly put out with all the noise and goings-on.

"You know," Kati said happily, sweeping them with a glance. "I love all of you. Even if you are the *nosiest* customers a body ever had."

"Well!" Vera huffed. "I never—"

"Yes, you have," Mr. Billings piped in, giving Vera a sidelong glance that caused her to blush.

Kati slid her arms around Luke and looked up into his face. She was so happy, she wanted the whole world to know it.

"Lucas Kane, I love you. And yes," she said with a wide smile, "I will marry you."

Luke gave a whoop of joy, picked her up and spun her around in a circle until she was nearly dizzy. "I love you, Kati," he yelled. "I love you."

"Can we go home, now?" Mr. Billings grumbled to Vera. "I've had enough excitement for one day."

"No, you haven't," Vera assured him saucily, flashing Kati a wink before taking his arm. "And no, we can't go home yet, we have to plan the wedding."

"Now!" Luke and Kati groaned in unison. "They're never going to let us be until we do," he told Kati, kissing her quick. "So let's get this over with so we can be alone. Let me handle it."

Kati nodded, finally realizing that never again would she have to handle everything alone. She had Luke, and together they would handle things.

"I think the bridal party should wear pink," Vera decided with an air of authority. "It's the perfect color for summer, don't you think?" she asked Bessie, who scowled.

"I ain't wearing no pink!" Bessie huffed. "I'll look like an inflated balloon. Let's wear blue."

"Blue!" Vera looked as if Bessie just announced she wanted to march down the aisle naked.

"I'm giving the bride away," Mr. Billings called and Wilfred whipped his head around.

"No, you're not," Wilfred protested. "*I'm* giving Kati away."

"Says who?" Mr. Billings demanded, shaking off Vera's restraining arm.

"Hold it!" Luke bellowed and everyone stopped to stare at him. "This is how we're going to work it. Wilfred, you and Mr. Billings can both give Kati away. One on each side. All right?" Both men looked at each other, grumbled softly, but finally nodded. Kati let out a sigh of relief.

"What about me, Luke?" Vera asked, clearly intent on being a part of the festivities.

"You and Bessie can be Kati's attendants. Vera, you can wear pink. Bessie, you can wear blue. All right?"

"Hey, what about me?" Kati asked, figuring she might as well get in on this since it was *her* wedding.

Luke turned to her with a smile. "You, my darling," he whispered, doing his best not to leer, "are not wearing *anything*. Is that all right with you?"

"That's fine with me." Kati grinned, pleased with his choice of wardrobe, and not caring who did what at her wedding, as long as Luke was there.

"Then it's settled," Luke announced, pulling Kati closer to him and pushing his way through the crowd so that they could have some privacy.

"Wait!" Mr. Billings yelled, causing Luke and Kati to come to an abrupt halt. He whispered something in Luke's ear and Kati leaned closer trying to hear, but Mr. Billings was too quick for her.

"What was that all about?" she asked Luke, her curiosity getting the best of her.

"Mr. Billings just asked me a favor."

"What kind of favor?" she asked suspiciously. "Don't tell me you told him he could bring that dog back into our diner," she cried in horror.

"No," Luke assured her.

"Then what?" Kati asked, and Bessie leaned closer so she wouldn't miss anything.

"Well, Mr. Billings just wanted to know if Beauregard could be in our wedding."

"What?" Bessie and Kati caroled in unison.

"Well," Luke said mischievously. "You've heard of flower girls?"

Kati and Bessie exchanged glances. "Yes," Kati said hesitantly.

"Well, I told Mr. Billings Beauregard could be the flower *dog*," Luke explained and Kati's mouth fell open.

"Lunatics," Bessie acknowledged. "Didn't I always tell you, Kati Rose?" she muttered, shaking her head and walking toward Wilfred. "Absolute lunatics!"

"A flower *dog*?" Kati echoed, as Luke guided her toward the stairs of her apartment. Laughing softly, she laid her head on Luke's shoulder. "Lucas Kane, what on earth am I going to do with you?"

Luke looked at her, his eyes soft and loving. "Come on upstairs, *Mabel*," he whispered wickedly. "And I'll be happy to show you."

Epilogue

Honey?" Luke whispered into the darkness. "Are you sleeping?"

"Sleeping?" Kati laughed, snuggling closer to her new husband. "No," she sighed dreamily. "I'm just gathering my strength."

Luke's warm chuckle filtered through the room. "Good," he drawled huskily. "You're going to need it. But right now, we have to talk." Luke sat up abruptly, pulling her with him.

"Talk!" Kati grumbled, adjusting the sheet more comfortably around her. "I don't want to talk, I want to—" Luke clamped his hand over her mouth and laughed softly.

"Kati Rose!" he scolded, his voice a husky whisper. "What would Bessie say if she heard you?"

"Who do you think gave me the idea?" Kati asked wickedly, snuggling closer.

"Kati?" The tone of his voice caused her to frown.

"Luke, what's wrong?"

"Now remember, I love you."

"I remember," she said, sliding her arm around his waist.

"Now promise you're not going to get mad?" His voice was so hopeful, she laughed softly.

"We've only been married six hours, Luke, how can I get mad?"

"Promise?"

"Promise," she assured him, feeling a bit suspicious. "What is it?"

"Do you remember when I sent Bessie home?"

"I remember," she said, wondering what Luke was getting at. "Bessie had the flu."

Luke's face split into a lopsided grin, and his eyes twinkled mischievously. "No, she didn't."

"Well, of course she did," Kati countered. "She missed two whole weeks of—" She stopped and her eyes rounded. "Lucas Kane, do you mean to tell me—" He nodded his head. "You two—you didn't—!" Her eyes widened. "You tricked me?" she cried incredulously.

"We sure did," he returned happily, not in the least bit remorseful. "We worked it out the morning I bought the new stove," he whispered. "Bessie knew you'd never accept me or my help as long as she was around. So she just conveniently got the flu so you'd be forced to rely on me."

"Lucas Kane!" Kati cried, giving him a poke in the ribs. "That was a terrible thing to do."

"I know." Luke laughed, grabbed her by the arms and tumbled her on top of him. "But it worked, didn't it?" he murmured, burying his face in the soft skin of her neck.

Squirming against him, Kati pushed her hair out of her face so she could look at him. "Yes, it worked." She laughed, adjusting herself more comfortably atop him. "Everything worked out just the way you planned, didn't it?"

"Well, almost everything," Luke commented, lifting his head to stare at the foot of the bed. Kati turned around and followed his gaze, trying not to laugh. Old Beauregard was flopped on the floor. His flower dog bonnet, complete with wilted pink and blue flowers was tied crookedly on his sleeping head. Beauregard gave a loud snore, sending the satin ribbon fluttering, and they both started laughing.

"I had meant this to be a honeymoon for two," Luke muttered. "But I guess Vera wanted to be sure you behaved."

"Me!" she cried, trying not to laugh. "You're the one poor Beauregard's supposed to protect! Luke! What are you doing?"

"You're not the only one Bessie gave a few tips to," he murmured softly pulling the sheet over their heads.

"Does this mean we're done talking now?" Kati inquired happily.

"It does," he whispered, groaning softly as he reacquainted himself with her softness.

"Good. I love you, *Kane*," she whispered, sliding her hands slowly across him.

"I love you, too, *Mabel*," Luke whispered, his breath shuddering through his lips. "But you talk too much!"

*   *   *   *   *

Take 4 Silhouette Desire novels
and a surprise gift
❧ FREE ❧

Then preview 6 brand-new Silhouette Desire novels—delivered to your door as soon as they come off the presses! If you decide to keep them, you pay just $2.24 each*—a 10% saving off the retail price, *with no additional charges for postage and handling!*

Silhouette Desire novels are not for everyone. They are written especially for the woman who wants a more satisfying, more deeply involving reading experience. Silhouette Desire novels take you beyond the others.

Start with 4 Silhouette Desire novels and a surprise gift absolutely FREE. They're yours to keep without obligation. You can always return a shipment and cancel at any time.

Simply fill out and return the coupon today!

* Plus 69¢ postage and handling per shipment in Canada.

Silhouette Romance™

Legendary Lovers Trilogy

BY DEBBIE MACOMBER....

ONCE UPON A TIME, in a land not so far away, there lived a girl, Debbie Macomber, who grew up dreaming of castles, white knights and princes on fiery steeds. Her family was an ordinary one with a mother and father and one wicked brother, who sold copies of her diary to all the boys in her junior high class.

One day, when Debbie was only nineteen, a handsome electrician drove by in a shiny black convertible. Now Debbie knew a prince when she saw one, and before long they lived in a two-bedroom cottage surrounded by a white picket fence.

As often happens when a damsel fair meets her prince charming, children followed, and soon the two-bedroom cottage became a four-bedroom castle. The kingdom flourished and prospered, and between soccer games and car pools, ballet classes and clarinet lessons, Debbie thought about love and enchantment and the magic of romance.

One day Debbie said, "What this country needs is a good fairy tale." She remembered how well her diary had sold and she dreamed again of castles, white knights and princes on fiery steeds. And so the stories of Cinderella, Beauty and the Beast, and Snow White were reborn....

Look for Debbie Macomber's *Legendary Lovers* trilogy from Silhouette Romance: *Cindy and the Prince* (January, 1988); *Some Kind of Wonderful* (March, 1988); *Almost Paradise* (May, 1988). Don't miss them!

SRT-1

COMING NEXT MONTH

#550 A MATTER OF HONOR—Brittany Young
FBI agent Tori Burton always got her man—but now the man she really wanted was Adam Danaro. Adam had agreed to help Tori with her latest case, but his family had always been on the wrong side of the law. Could Tori trust him with her life...and her heart?

#551 THE BEWITCHING HOUR—Jennifer Mikels
T.J. Hawkins had left Samantha Tyler years ago to become a football star. Now that he was back, Samantha was determined not to get hurt again. But T.J. had learned from his mistakes—he knew he had to prove to Samantha that the time for their love had finally come....

#552 HOUSE CALLS—Terry Essig
Andrea Conrades was not about to let Gregory Rennolds, M.D., railroad her into marriage—even if he could prove the chemistry between them with one devastating kiss....

#553 SEASON OF THE HEART—Pat Warren
When journalist Laura Franklin decided to get the scoop on a new Colorado ski lodge, she'd expected an icy reception from its media-hating owner, former Olympic medalist Dan Kramer. She never guessed Dan would warm to her. If she returned his feelings, would she be skating on thin ice?

#554 AUTHOR'S CHOICE—Elizabeth August
If Melinda Oliver wanted to keep the custody of her niece and nephew she'd have to find a temporary husband—fast! Handsome adventure writer John Medwin was willing, but what would he do when he discovered Melinda had concocted a story of her own—a romance between the two of them?

#555 CINDY AND THE PRINCE—Debbie Macomber
(Book One of the LEGENDARY LOVERS Trilogy)
Cindy Territo believed in fairy tales—in one night she'd convinced hard-headed executive Thorndike Prince that she was his real-life Cinderella. Cindy was in love, but how was she going to keep her prince from discovering that she was also the person who cleaned his office?

AVAILABLE THIS MONTH: